THE COLDEST BILLIONAIRE OUT THE DIRTY SOUTH

BY:
TIECE

ISLANDE "REMY" PIERRE

"Ahhh Papi, right there," Sasha let out as she rode my dick backwards. I slapped her on the ass, grinding so hard from the bottom, I could feel the insides of her stomach rumbling.

"Islaaaande," Lisa loudly moaned. "Yesss! Eat this pussy baby; it's all yours."

I palmed Lisa's butt cheeks with both hands, sliding and dipping my tongue in and out of her creamy goodness. I had one bad bitch ridin' my face and the other ridin' my pipe. This was what I called living my best life and enjoying the best of both worlds.

"Shit, I love you, Islande," Lisa seductively sang, rocking back and forth on my mouth. I absorbed her sweet juices like a sponge, swirling my tongue around her succulent lips. Fat ma tasted like she missed daddy and, damn, daddy missed her too. Finger fuckin' while devouring her temple had Lisa with the shakes. I could feel her clit throbbin' and, just as I figured, she gushed pours of raindrops down my throat. Once I'd gulped all I could, I literally tossed her lightweight ass over to the side and switched positions.

"Bend over," I told Sasha. She wasted no time getting on all fours. I started pounding her from the back, slipping my dick out and slapping her ass with it, then drilling it back in. Gazing in Lisa's eyes as she played in her pussy, I smiled while biting the corner of my bottom lip, still humpin'. I looked down, easing out a bit, then spittin' on my wood before piercing Sasha's sleek insides again. Ol' girl was now just semi-wet. I could tell she was giving out, but I'd popped a Perc and drank a half bottle of Clase Azul Gold tequila. I was lit. This kinda shit was nothing new. Although Lisa was a regular, she'd been gettin' the dick for almost two years now. Sasha was her best friend. Every once in a while, she didn't mind sharing, or at least she knew what I liked and wanted to keep me locked in. Hell, it was working, even though I had no real feelings for her. It was just her sex drive that turned me on.

After almost two hours of watching them eat each other out, wild foreplay, fucking, sucking, slurping and banging the headboard loose, I pulled my nine, thick inches out and started jacking it. They knew what time it was. Both crawled over and began suckin' at the same time. My head fell back, as my eyes rolled from the intensifying sensation rushing through my veins. My heart began to rapidly beat like it was about to come out my chest.

"Open wide," I demanded, hosing the back of their tonsils simultaneously as they swallowed while licking their lips to make sure that the liquid gold wasn't wasted. "Ahhh," I groaned. Shit felt so good.

"You sound like you needed that." Sasha grinned.

"Shit, I did."

"You lyin'," Lisa chimed in as she slid off the bed. "You get pussy every night of the week."

"Nah, that ain't true. Even you should know that. I *could* get pussy every night of the week, but my life don't just revolve around fuckin'."

"Yeah, you have business to tend to. Ain't no way this twelve-million-dollar condo is paying for itself," Sasha chimed in.

I nodded at her. "At least you know."

"Sasha, be quiet. You always tryna dick ride."

"Um, I don't think I was just trying. I definitely did that. Am I right, Islande?"

I grinned. "Yea, you did that."

Lisa slick rolled her eyes and headed in the bathroom suite to wash up. The second the shower turned on, Sasha started.

"I don't know why she's always actin' like that. If she don't want us fuckin', she shouldn't invite me to join in."

I shrugged. For some reason, Lisa had just recently started this weird behavior. She first walked in with my name tatted on her titty. What the fuck? Bitch got a whole man. Then it definitely seemed like she was a lil' jealous of the one person she bought in to join us. I mean, the way Sasha sucked and fucked me, I guess if I was her, I'd feel a way too. Not that I cared for either of them like that but,' if I had to choose, Lisa's ass would be knocked the fuck out the box. I smiled at Sasha with a shake of the head.

"Don't let that bother you. I like when you join us. From the way you was munchin' on Lisa's asshole, I'd say she loves your company too. She might get a lil' territorial from time to time but, like always, she gets over it."

"You're right." She smiled. "I probably need to join her before she thinks we're in here on round six."

"I'm burnt-out baby. Ain't no mo' rounds left in me tonight."

Sasha laughed. "Shit, you got my coochie lips fat as hell. My shit so swollen, my pee might not be able to come out now."

I laughed. "You funny as fuck."

"Shit, I'm for real." She chuckled. "I see why Lisa all in love with you. I been trying not to fall but you fuck a bitch so good, we can't help it."

I shook my head. "Listen ma, I'm not the one you fall in love with. I break backs and hearts. If you find yourself getting in too deep, then it might be best if you don't come in," I told her, especially being that I had already contemplated leaving Lisa alone. All that *I love you* shit while we was fuckin' wasn't it. I knew she'd fallen a long time ago, but she always held her composure. Now suddenly, she wanted to cry out her love. Maybe it was more about fuckin' with Sasha but, either way, I ain't like it.

"You coming?"

I grabbed my Bottega boxer briefs and put 'em on. "Nah, y'all got that."

"Come ooon," she sang. "We love when you shower with us."

"I'm good, ma. I told you, Ion want no smoke."

She laughed like I'd said a joke. "You're gonna miss the show."

"I believe I caught all the show I needed."

"Ok, I tried," she teased, walking in the bathroom. I admired her Latino mix of curly hair, witty personality, cute face and a body that Dr. Miami had put his stamp on. She was certainly a bad bitch but still not for me.

As they showered, I headed out the bedroom and down the spiraling staircase that led me straight into the white and gray color schemed kitchen. Running my fingers across the smooth marble countertop, I made my way to the sub-zero refrigerator. My throat was dry as hell. I grabbed an Alkaline water and turned it up. Damn, I needed this shit in my system. I drank a lil' more while thinking about the events that had just taken place. I always enjoyed nights in like this. After calling it quits for the umpteenth time with Regan, it was always either strip clubs, bad bitches back-to-back, or Lisa with Sasha to fulfill my lonely cravings.

A peaceful smile crossed my face, as I glanced around my lavishly decked-out, open floor plan of expensive décor and exotic furniture. To this day, it was hard to believe that a nigga like me made it out the country. Literally, I'd moved out of Georgia and to New York, following my dreams. From New York, I moved to New Hampshire on some bigger, deeper shit. To make it this far was by the grace of God. The odds were stacked against me from the age of ten when I lost my dad and, then, my mom. Being raised in a four-bedroom house with two siblings and four cousins wasn't easy, but my grandmother and my aunt held down the fort and did the best they could. We were wild as fuck though, all of us in our own ways. We stayed getting kicked out of school to fights that led to shoot-outs, which caused some of the craziest beef in the streets. We sold dope, smoked plenty of weed, and was known as the family that didn't fuck around. My turning point was killing a nigga by the time I was twenty-one but, because my attorney proved it was self-defense, I got off with a slap on the wrist. However, I knew I needed to make a change or my grandmother would either be grieving over me or visiting me in prison. Either way, the outcome wasn't a good one.

I buckled down and took the road less dangerous. I enrolled in a technical college and allowed my heart to steer me in the direction of my father's path. He was a computer scientist that designed software for a small-time company who ended up benefiting abundantly after his death. Somehow, his gift and talents trickled down to me. After toying around long enough creating app after app, I finally created an interactive dating app that allowed the users to design their own avatars to meet singles. A major plus about the app were the required background checks that were privately added to their profiles. If asked, they could show it to whomever they were dating. These dates were meant to evolve outside of their online communications and, according to stats, the majority of them did. I named the app *A Royal Love*.

Long story short, some savvy entrepreneurs got a whiff of what I'd been working on and offered me a check so immense that it was hard for me to deny it. Not only did I still have stock in the app, but I was also making money in my sleep, lots of money.

"What you doing?" Lisa asked as she walked up behind me with my phone in her hand. "You missed three calls."

"Ok, thanks. Y'all leaving?"

"Yea, we're headed out. I'll call you later this week," she said, kissing me softly on the lips.

"See ya next time." Sasha waved. I was sure she wished she could kiss me too, but Lisa would have a fit.

"A'ight Sasha." I smiled.

"I'll lock up," Lisa added.

"Ok, ma."

I held my phone, looking at the caller ID. The missed calls were from my 1st cousin Joe, also my right-hand man. I frowned. He knew I was laid up with two bad bitches. Plus, he claimed he was about to do the same, even though he should've been laid up with his baby mama tryna win her fully back. So, I couldn't understand why he was calling. Just as I was getting ready to call him back, my phone rang again. This time, it was Nana. My heart instantly dropped. If Roselee Pierre was making a personal call at this hour, something had happened.

"Nana," I nervously answered.

"It's Maddy, nephew."

"Auntie," I deeply sighed. "Why you calling me from Nana's phone?"

"Well—um—" she hesitated, but I could hear her crying as she tried talking.

"Something wrong with her?!" I quickly questioned, heart beating fast as fuck.

"No, but—"

"But what?!"

"It's Lovely, James, and Wesley."

My eyes stretched wide the fuck open. "What happened?" I asked, hands now shaking nervously, almost to a point that I dropped the phone. "Is my sister ok?"

"Well, uh—no—"

"What you mean no, Auntie?!"

She cried out, almost choking on her words. "She and James were killed tonight in an apparent, targeted shooting. Wesley is here in the hospital, but he's stable."

I felt full and faint at the same time. I didn't know if I was hearing her right but, if she was saying what I thought she said, my sister and my 1st cousin James were dead.

"Nephew!" she called out in between the groans of painful tears. "Mama has also been admitted just so they can control her blood pressure. She's been given a calmer."

I heard everything auntie was saying, but I was stuck. I was fuckin' stuck!

"Nephew!" she cried out.

The room started to spin as my vision grew blurry. Who in the fuck had nuts that big to fuck with my family? At that time, I broke down dropping the phone beside me as I fell to my knees. I cried out like a baby. I could also hear my auntie wailing through the speaker of the phone. This shit was heart wrenching. I couldn't believe it. I just couldn't believe it. I didn't know how much time had gone by but, when I finally picked the phone back up, it was only one thing I could say.

"Tell Nana and everybody else to stay strong. We're coming home."

***

I pulled up to the private jet, noticing my personal assistant was already there waiting on me. She literally got paid just to be on call when I needed her. She walked over to the car tapping on the dark tinted windows of my black-on-black Aston Martin Victor.

"You have bags, Boss?"

I simply popped the trunk. After grabbing my luggage, she headed for the jet just as Joe pulled beside me and parked. I looked over only trying to imagine what he was dealing with himself. James was his older brother. We both had lost siblings. Just thinking about it had me sick to my fuckin' stomach. The fact that we hadn't stepped on Georgia's soil in over ten years was one thing, but to go back on these terms was another. I tried gathering my composure before getting out the car, but thoughts of me and Lovely's last conversation continued to play in my mind. I couldn't believe that I had just spoken to her over the phone while she, James and Wesley were heading to the Chinese restaurant to grab some late-night take-out. The conversation replayed over and over in my mind.

"Lovely Pierre, what do I owe the pleasure?"

She laughed in the phone. "Islande Pierre, the only nigga I know that mimics his name very well."

I laughed. "Quit saying that."

"You're a loner, my nigga. Just like a fuckin' Island. The only person that hangs around yo' ass all the time is Joe, Marla and that fine ass nerdy muthafucka—"

"Santana!" Wesley called out in the background with laughter.

"Yea, Santana," she laughed.

"Wassup, my favorite cousin!" Wesley said aloud.

"Wassup boy. Y'all staying outta trouble on that end?"

"You know how we do my nigga," James' raspy, deep voice chimed in. "The Pierre's and the Baptiste's don't fuck around. We run this shit."

I grinned. My cousin James was a fool with it. "Oh, what up J the gangster? You still flying out here next week?"

"Hell yea, my dirty cousin," he answered.

"Nigga, you lyin'. I can't get yo' ass to leave Georgia for shit," I laughed.

"Shiiid, I need a break. You know it gets crazy round here from time to time."

"With the line of work y'all in, I could see why," I said. "Bring Wesley with you. Y'all niggas act like leaving Georgia is a bad thing. Shit, New Hampshire is the life," I teased but was very serious.

"Nigga, it's cold as fuck there. Especially this time of year. Ian coming," Wesley chuckled in a serious tone.

"For niggas to be so hard, y'all scared of a lil' ice storm and cold weather?" I grinned.

"Hell yea!" Wesley answered.

"It's the truth though, boy. But I'm still coming for 'bout a week," James slid in.

"A'ight, I'ma see. Anyway, where y'all headed, ridin' round like the three muthafuckin' Stooges?"

Lovely laughed. *"To get some Chinese food. Wesley ol' greedy ass—"*

"Girl stop," Wesley joked.

"Y'all must be on a late-night binge?"

"Yea, we just got a shipment in, so you know it's all work, no play."

"Cuzn' listen, her ass used to be ghost but, now, it's all work, no play since she done broke up with—"

"Hush Wesley!" Lovely shouted.

"Who she fuckin' with now, Cuz?" I nosily pondered.

"Nobody," Lovely cut in. *"Hush Wesley!"*

"Aye, hang up the phone right quick" James said out of nowhere.

"Why nigga? You see me talkin' to my brother."

"I know that—" he hesitated. *"Pay attention,"* he said, as the car got quiet.

"Bro, we gon' call you back."

"Why? What's going on?"

"I'll call you back," she said again. *"Love you."*

"A'ight. Love you too," I responded and ended the call.

As tears rolled down my face, I never thought that would be the last time I'd hear her and James' voice. A light tap on my window brought me back to reality.

"You good, Boss?"

Quickly wiping my tears, I answered from behind my window. "Yea." Seconds later, I stepped out the car.

"I tapped on Joe's window, but he didn't respond."

"It's ok, Marla. You can board the jet. Tell the pilot we're coming." As Marla walked off, I made my way around to Joe's driver door. "Joe, come on." I couldn't see behind his tint, but I could only imagine he was having a moment like me. "Joe!" I called out again.

His door eased open as he got out the car. The second his feet touched the ground, we wrapped our arms around each other. I hadn't felt this much sorrow since losing my father and my auntie, Joe's mother. So, I knew exactly what he was feeling. Here we were again, having lost two people near and dear to our hearts. Here we were once again, leaning heavily on each other to get through this gut-wrenching pain except, this time, we weren't kids. We'd already dealt with loss in the most challenging way. Now, we were dealing with death on a whole new level.

"Somebody killed 'em!" he cried out.

"I know Joe. I know," I sadly responded, trying to be strong for him but, deep down, I wanted to lose it. It seemed like forever as we stood in the still of the night under the bright stars, as snow began to lightly drizzle. "We gotta go Joe."

"I don't know if I can do this again."

"You can," I assured him. "We're gonna get through this together, as a family. Nana needs us, Auntie Maddy needs us, everybody else needs us. We have to find out what happened."

Joe gathered his composure, slowly backing out of our embrace. "You're right. We gotta go back."

At that moment, I could see the look in his eyes. I knew what time it was. "You brought anything?"

"Nah," he replied. "I'll grab some things when I get there."

"Ok. Lock up and let's go."

As we boarded the private jet, Marla greeted us. "Y'all good?" she sincerely asked.

"Yea, you can let the pilot know we're ready to go."

"Ok." She politely nodded.

In no time, we were getting ready for take-off. Marla joined us. "Should I have the cars transported back to your house? Joe's house?"

"You can have my Aston sent back to my house, but have the bulletproof Mercedes Maybach sent to Georgia."

Joe looked over at me, almost with a gleam in his eyes. "Marla, have my car transported back home, as well. But I need the Wrangler transported to Georgia."

"The souped up Jeep Wrangler Rubicon? That's your lil' boy toy."

"I know. I feel like it's time to play."

I nodded my head. "Touché."

We weren't the average family. We were wealthy but the riches didn't come overnight. Of course, what Joe and I did was legal and legit. Our siblings did a bit of both, legal and illegal shit. It was true, you could take a nigga out the country, but you could never take the country out a nigga. That saying definitely described my family to a T. Even though we all lived the life of luxury, some of us still chose to roam the streets for notoriety. We were well respected; our last names carried weight. Most of it was for unpleasant reasons, nevertheless. So, for someone to gun down my people like they were nobodies had me baffled. I knew it had been a long time since I'd showed face, but that was for their own good. Now, they'd awakened the demon in me, and I was ready to destroy anything in my path that had something to do with James and Lovely's death. Bitches in Georgia had better sleep lightly because a real nigga was coming back home.

ISLANDE "REMY" PIERRE

Two hours later, we'd touched down in Gainesboro, Georgia, the deer capital of the world. With a population of around sixty-five thousand, it was still considered to be one of the biggest cities in Georgia because of its vast country acreage. The air smelled different getting off the jet. It was definitely a cold, late January morning but no snow, like it was in New Hampshire. Hell, Georgia never really got snow, at least not in the twenty-two years I lived here.

Marla had a driver already waiting for us. Our first stop was the hospital and, while we were seeing what was going on there, Marla would be heading to a hotel to get us checked in. Of course, we had plenty of room at Nana's six-thousand square foot estate but, for some of the shit I'd have going on, I didn't need to be around Nana's house for that. Plus, I liked my space. I'd gotten accustomed to it. Of course, I'd visit daily but I really didn't feel the need to stay there.

The driver pulled up to the hospital, as my heart sank deep in my chest. Just the ride over had me feeling a lil' antsy. Things had changed in ten years. I mean, drastically changed. Stores were here that weren't here before. Shopping plazas were throughout the drive over. Known restaurants had now been built to elevate the city. We even passed two newly built luxury hotels that would surely accommodate my needs during our stay. I could see why my cousins enjoyed being here. It didn't look as boring of a town as it did back when we were growing up.

"You need me to come in for a lil' bit?"

"No, Marla. But thanks for asking. We'll be ok. Right, Joe?"

Joe shrugged but nodded his head. I could see the pain in his eyes. I wondered if he saw that same look in mine.

"Ok, Boss. I'll head to the hotel and make sure that everything is as you'd both want it to be by the time y'all get there. Again, I am so sorry for y'all's loss. I'm praying for your family."

"Thanks for everything Marla."

"Thanks Marla," Joe finally said. Those were the first words he'd spoken since leaving New Hampshire's skies.

We stepped out the 2022 black Tahoe and headed inside the hospital. I couldn't lie; I wasn't in a rush, and it didn't seem like Joe was either. We dreaded this return, simply because it wasn't a pleasant one. The reason we never came home, not even to visit, was evident. For one, we had become known as the town gangsters, the city bullies. We took no shit and played the cards that were dealt to us, whether that was good or bad. We left the city to end that stigma. We left to better ourselves. We knew the world was bigger than Gainesboro and, with the blessing of Nana, we sought out to explore and conquer, no matter where we ended up at.

The hospital itself was only two floors. The second floor had been added in the years that I was away. We got in the elevator and headed straight up to the second floor. Upon stepping off the elevator, we walked straight into the waiting room and was met by Josette and Royal. Josette rushed over to Joe, and Royal rushed over to me. They both fell in our arms crying. Joe and I stood hugging our sisters and trying to comfort them, while needing the same energy from them. The moment was so surreal and still unbelievable. Tensions were high and we all were on edge.

"Where is Nana? How's Wesley doing?"

"I just left out the room with Wesley. He was shot in the butt twice and the hand once. Both were clean shots. I believe they're discharging him today," Josette explained. "Aunt Maddy is with Nana, but they're discharging her too once her vitals are stable and she's fully calmed down. Seeing you and bro will help with that, I'm sure."

"Yea, I'm sure. Can we go see them?"

"They can only have one visitor right now because of Covid. But when Auntie comes out, one of you can go in," Josette replied. "Gaelle is in the room with Wesley. You know she ain't leaving that nigga's side too funny."

"Him and Gaelle still hanging in there," I approvingly nodded, thinking that Wesley was no saint by a long shot, but he loved himself some Gaelle and she loved herself some him. It was like they were made for each other.

"Who would do this to them?" Royal asked in tears. Clearly, she was broken. Josette was a lil' stronger than Royal. Royal was the baby of our entire crew. However, she moved like a Pierre. The pretty face would fool a bitch. She could get down with the best of 'em. I'd seen her in action a couple of times. I knew what she was capable of.

I continued to hug her. "I don't know sis but, when I find out, it's gon' be some smoke in the city."

"I'm killing first and fuck questions later."

"Joe, let's just let cooler heads prevail for now. Y'all just came home. We're happy y'all here," Josette acknowledged in between tears. "But in no way will whoever did this not deal with the consequences behind it."

"In no fuckin' way will they get away with this," Joe settled.

Just being here was eating us up, so I finally asked the question that I dreaded an answer to. "Can we see them, Lovely and James?"

"Auntie was able to identify them about an hour ago. I don't know if y'all can or not, but you'd have to go to the coroner's office to see," Josette explained.

"I don't wanna see them like that," Royal cried.

In my heart, that was definitely too much for me to see, but a part of me had to. "Do y'all know what happened?"

"From what we're told, they were parking in front of the Chinese restaurant when a white sedan pulled up beside them and started shooting. James was able to escape the vehicle, shooting back. However, the shot to his head ended his life instantly. The restaurant has footage. The cops say they'll look over it and see what they can find out."

"So, there is footage?" I pondered.

"Yea." Josette nodded.

"Auntie said it was targeted, though."

"Why would Auntie say that?" Joe asked.

"Because Lovely had mentioned that someone had been threatening her."

"Who?" I asked, but Aunt Maddy stepped in the waiting room and ran over to hug us. She was a strong lady, having also dealt with the blow of losing her sister twenty-three years prior. However, this hit even closer to home being that Wesley was her only son.

"How are y'all doing?" she asked, looking us over. "Y'all look good."

"Thanks Auntie. We're doing about as well as expected. This has certainly caught us all by surprise, but we're not leaving until somebody pays for this."

"Please, don't come back and get yourselves in trouble. This city ain't the city it was before y'all left. Things have changed and newcomers are running the town. The last thing I want is for mama to have to deal with more than she can handle. Losing James and Lovely is like losing her daughters— My sisters, all over again." She explained. "Mama raised y'all. Y'all made her stronger during one of the lowest points in her life. Right now, she's going through it. So, whatever you do, don't stress her any more than she already is."

"We won't," I assured her. "But, are y'all safe? If you feel this was a targeted shooting, do you think they'll come back for more blood?"

"No, I honestly don't. I just think that your sister had gotten way in over her head. But we'll talk about that later. Now is not the time. We're all grieving. Let's put them to rest and then find out answers. What's done has been done; none of us can take it back. I'm just glad to have y'all home. We really need y'all at a time like this."

"You're right Auntie." I understood with a genuine nod. "Can I go see Nana?"

"Yes, please do. She in room 214, down the hall to the right. She was resting when I left. I'm sure it's the medicine they gave her. But she'll feel so much better to see you when she awakens," she said, then directed her attention at Joe. "Come here Joe. Talk to your auntie. I've missed you."

"I've missed you too," Joe responded, as he and Maddy sat down beside each other. I knew what she was doing. She didn't want us to retaliate and, even though we'd left that life behind, we couldn't let this slide.

"Royal, I'm 'bout to go see Nana. Will you be alright?"

"Yea." She nodded, still crying. But, she too was strong and, somehow, we'd get through this trying time together.

"I'll be back."

I headed down the hall, looking for the room number. My heart ached for my Nana. She was the matriarch of our family, the glue that held us together. But she'd gone through some hurtful things in her life.

I nervously entered the room. The last thing I wanted to witness was her going back down that emotional rollercoaster. A part of me was glad that she was sleeping peacefully. This was definitely the only way to keep her sane at a time like this. She had to have been going through it. I knew how I felt, so I could only imagine the pain that she was dealing with.

After sitting in the room for nearly an hour, I called Marla. She answered on the first ring.

"Hello."

"You good?"

"Yea, I got you and Joe a separate suite for the week. Do you know how long y'all will be staying here?"

"Nah, not right now, but it might be for a while."

"Well, I can always extend the stay. How is everyone?"

"Heartbroken," I answered. "We never would've expected something like this to happen."

"I know y'all didn't. I'm just so sorry to hear about it. I have three siblings and I wouldn't know what I'd do if anything happened to either of them."

"Let's pray y'all live very long, happy lives because this shit here ain't it. I literally feel sick to my stomach."

"Let me handle things for you and the family. You know I got you. I'll call around and set up arrangements—that's if you want the help. I don't wanna overstep my boundaries—"

"No, you're not overstepping your boundaries. I appreciate everything you've done and all you continue to do. This will relieve me and my family some."

"Anything for you, Boss. I just want to be here for you and Joe as much as I can. I don't mind staying out here for the duration of the time that y'all are here. It's not like I have a whole lot going on in New Hampshire besides working for you," she teased. That only meant that she didn't have a man to run back to.

"I appreciate it, Marla. I'll text over some things that you can look into once I speak with Nana and Auntie. We gon' ride back with them, so you don't have to worry about that. Order whatever you want and have it brought to the room. The city has grown quite a bit, so you might wanna explore this uprising country scenery," I teased.

"What's a good place to eat around here?"

"Check out either Big Chick or Lil' Chick. They always had the best chicken, burgers and fries. I've heard Nana talking about 'em recently. She said that nothing has changed. Their food always taste the same."

"I'm lookin' 'em up as we speak. I'm so hungry. I can have them deliver y'all some food at the hospital if you'd like. Oh wait, they don't open until eleven. That's over an hour away."

"Damn, I forgot about that. But, hey, check out Fran's Breakfast Bar. That's a spot that Royal invested in a couple of years back. Her homegirl, Fran, owns the joint. Tell her I sent you. Let them tell it, Fran got some real skills in the kitchen. Royal says the breakfast is good as hell. Of course, I gotta check it out while we're here."

"I'm looking it up right now as well. But did y'all want something?"

"I don't even have an appetite and I'm sure that no one else has one either. But thanks for asking."

"Are they keeping your cousin and your grandmother in the hospital?"

"I believe they're letting both of them go home today. My cousin didn't have any major injuries, although I'm sure the whole ordeal was traumatic."

"I know right."

"Nana is resting right now but, as long as her vitals stay stable, then she'll be fine."

"Ok, that's good to hear."

"I know right. We've already dealt with enough, and now this. I just pray that we all have the strength because this is a lot. I lost my sister and my cousin," I said through a choked tone. But I sucked it up. I didn't need Nana waking up to me having a breakdown. I had to be strong for her.

"I don't even have the words to comfort you the way you really need it, but I'm praying for you. You'll get through this. You're a strong person yourself. I admire that about you."

"Thanks Marla."

"Always, Boss."

"Anyway, let me get off this phone. Nana's moving around a little. She's probably about to wake up."

"Ok. Call me when you leave there."

"I will," I responded, ending the call. I stood up and walked closer to Nana's bedside. Her eyes twitched under her eyelids and, then, they just popped open. She stared at me; I stared back.

"Remy—you made it."

"Yes, Nana, I'm here."

"Joe?"

"He's here in the waiting room."

She smiled. "Thank the Lord y'all made it." Then, out of nowhere, she started crying. "My babies are gone."

"I know, Nana."

"They're gone."

"I know," I repeated, leaning over in the bed and hugging her.

"Remy, don't y'all leave me."

"I'm not going anywhere Nana. I'm here to stay for a while. You gotta calm down though. I know this is hard. We're all shocked by this, but you gotta calm down. The last thing we need is you getting sick."

"I don't know if I have the strength for this one. It's too much. I'm getting old, Remy. This is too much," she cried.

"I know," I told her. Her eyes seemed heavy like she was still sleepy. I was sure it was because of the medicine and, at this point, I felt they needed to send a prescription of this stuff home with her. "Nana, rest. Just get you some rest. Let us handle everything else. We got this."

She laid there, staring off into space. Her eyes glanced over my way a couple of times, but I could tell she was out of it. She looked tired in the face. I wiped her eyes, as she closed them shut.

"I'm so glad you're home," she whispered.

I smiled on the outside, but the pain of me being here had my stomach in knots. I sat down in the chair next to the bed, as Nana softly snored. To hear her say she didn't have the strength this time almost broke me down. Losing her husband was something she saw coming but losing everybody else that was dear to her heart wasn't. I thought about my mother and my aunt Nadia. I thought about my father and the last real moments I spent with them. Suddenly, all of those memories rushed back, and that devastating day twenty-three years ago replayed in my mind.

"Islande, go get your father. Joseph acting a fool again."

"Why is Uncle Joe always acting crazy?"

"Because he's a sick man. War done a number on him, son."

"Well, he need to stop and think sometimes before he reacts. Dad says if he does that, then he wouldn't be having so many fits."

"Wouldn't that be nice," she uttered, rubbing her big belly. "But right now, I need your father to go pick up Nadia and the kids."

"Why can't auntie just drive over here? You know daddy outside working and he don't like to be bothered when he's in the shed.

"Boy, go get your father and stop talking so much."

"Okaaay." I ran outside in the backyard where dad was in the shed doing some work on his computer. No telling what he was cooking up. "Dad, mama said to come here. Uncle Joe acting crazy again."

"I just hung with Joe a couple of hours ago and told him to take his medicine," Dad fussed as he followed me back in the house.

"Ramirez, baby, we need to go pick up Nadia and the kids. Joseph over there acting a fool and, this time, she's leaving him until he gets himself together."

"That's the best thing she could do right now because he's been at this for over a year. I don't know if he'll change any time soon, if at all. He needs counseling—"

"And to take his medicine," Mom added as she stood up and grabbed her purse. "You know I would be damaged beyond repair if something happened to my twin sister."

"I know, dear. But, since you're already thirty-nine weeks pregnant and due anytime now with our little Royal princess, I need you to stay home. I'll pick up Nadia and the kids and we'll come right back here."

"You sure? I can ride with you. I don't have to get out. I just need to lay my eyes on her. While on the phone, she said that he grabbed her by the neck of her shirt when she told him that she was staying with us for a while. James and Lil Joe started kicking him. Of course, he turned her loose but then wanted to spank the boys for taking up for her. I don't know what's going on with him, but he's never spanked those kids, nor has he ever put his hands on my sister in any kind of way that was harmful. He's starting to scare me."

"Yea, that is unusual. But, again, you don't need to be around that. You can see her when we get back. Ok."

Mama frowned with a disapproving expression.

"Yea mama, who gon' be here with us if you leave?" I asked. A part of me didn't want her to go either. I didn't like when my Uncle Joe acted loud and crazy.

"Remy, you know your auntie lives right behind us. She can watch you and Lovely til we get back. Matter of fact, go outside and play with Wesley. Do something constructive with yo' lil' life." She teased with a loving smile.

"Speaking of Maddy, she can also watch you because you're not going. Now, sit down," Dad insisted. *"I'll be back."*

"Dad!" I called out, as he glanced over his shoulder at me. I just stared at him. *"Never mind."*

"Alright son. I'll be back. I love y'all."

We said we loved him too and, then, he was gone. Who would've thought he wouldn't have ever returned? Unfortunately, he wasn't the only parent I had who left me. That day traumatized us, but somehow, we managed to grow closer through the pain. Now, twenty-three years later, a similar devastation had happened again on the exact day and only time would tell how this one was going to end.

JOSEPH "JOE" BAPTISTE JR.

I woke up with a banging headache, having stayed up all night drinking and playing board games with my family as we caught up on lost time. It was crazy how ten years of me being gone had passed, yet our bond hadn't changed. The love was still the same, if not stronger. The only thing missing was the void in our hearts of missing James and Lovely being there.

I didn't get to see James often, but we talked on the phone a lot. We also did video calls anytime he wanted to show off his new jewelry, a new bitch, or to let me speak with my twin nephews and three nieces. I sighed, thinking about his offspring. Just that alone took me back to losing both our parents damn near in a similar way, just on another level. My heart ached for them.

Hearing that James was able to escape the car and shoot back, hitting one of the people in the drive-by shooting, didn't surprise me. James was a straight up thug. He took no shit. He was known as the heartless one. *The crazy Baptiste boy* was his nickname throughout the hoods. A lot of that aggression came from losing our parents. He never was able to deal with the loss constructively. At times, I didn't know who was worse, him or Remy. They were the two that ran closely together with Wesley and me as the back-up crew. They handled business; we made sure nobody interfered with that business.

Then, one day, James and an opp name Rudy Cannon had words. The beef was already thick in the streets between us and them. Ironically, they had a clan like we did. They were known as the tough guys that always wanted all the smoke, even when we were in school. However, Remy knocked out Rudy, the older brother and, from that day, a silent truce was formed. They stayed out our way and, well, we stayed out theirs. Until—

James and Tony Cannon, the youngest brother, butted heads over a dice game. Tony wanted smoke because James had beat him out his money. Long story short, shots were fired at James by Tony, but James shot back, hitting Tony in the leg. Remy was on the scene and was trying to get James to the car, however, Rudy came out of nowhere and grazed Remy on the arm. Remy returned fire and killed Rudy on the spot. That had to be one of the most talked about gun blazing nights in Gainesboro, Georgia.

Rudy was really the leader of the pack and, once he was dead, the beef also died down. Nana never felt like it was over and wanted James and Remy to move in with her distant half-sister who lived in New York and attend school. Remy didn't put up much of a fight after he beat his murder charges. I believed he saw the light and wanted out of the foolishness. James refused to leave and so that was my chance to haul ass with Remy. Once I left Georgia, I never looked back. As I laid in bed with my mind still on overload, my cell phone rang.

"Yo," I answered.

"Morning love," Iesha said. "How are you feeling?"

"I'm ok or as 'bout as ok as I'll get."

"Awww, I really wanna be there for you."

"I know, but I don't know what's going on yet. The last thing I need is for you to get caught up in something I have no control over."

"So, the people that did this to your family is still out for more?"

"I don't know. I hope not. It's only been three days and we haven't found out much. Actually, we're laying low, even though I'm sure word is out that me and Remy are back in town. We didn't exactly leave on good terms ten years ago. So, you know how that is."

"I understand babe."

"People around here knows us. They're likely feeling the heat. Whoever did this is either hiding out, skipped town or is gonna boldly make their presence known. Not to a point that it identifies them as the shooters, but we'll find out."

"And then y'all go straight to the police and have their asses locked the fuck up."

"Babe, we're not snitches. That's one thing we don't do around here, especially my family."

"So, y'all are just gonna sit back and let them get away with this shit?"

"I didn't say that, did I?"

"Unt-unt—nope— you don't need to be gettin' caught up in no trouble down there. I need you to make it back home. Our daughters need you."

I rested my head back on the pillow. Thoughts of my twin girls growing up without me was not an option. I loved my family, without a doubt.

"Hello? Joe, you hear me?"

"Yea, babe. I hear you."

"Well, you need to make it back home. I'm not playing about that."

"I will. Don't worry yourself."

"By the way since I've given you a lil' time, where were you the night that happened?"

"Huh?"

"Huh?" she mocked with a smack of the lips. I already knew where this shit was going.

"I don't know what you're talking 'bout."

"Joe, don't play with me. That night you got the call and had to fly out, where were you? I had called you twice and you didn't answer, nor did you respond back to my text."

"I was at Remy's house."

Silence crept in for a few seconds. "Joe—"

"Iesha, I don't have time for this shit."

"But I do, dammit."

"And I don't, dammit," I responded back. "You trippin' right now."

"You know we're already trying to get back on the right track. You said if I took you back, you'd do better and not fuck around on me."

"I know what I said and I'm telling you now isn't the time for this. I ain't fucking around, haven't fucked around and ain't thinking about it woman. Chill out."

"Ok, if I leave your slick haired ass this time, don't beg me to take you back."

I grinned in the phone. "Girl, I ain't never begged yo' ass."

"Lies you tell," she laughed.

We had a moment of jokes and chuckles. This was what I loved about Iesha. She was not only beautiful and the mother of my daughters, but she had a way about herself that was graceful and witty. She told quirky jokes that made me laugh and, even though I had been somewhat of an asshole boyfriend, she stayed down no matter what. I definitely had thoughts of proposing one day; and after losing my loved ones, those thoughts were starting to feel like I shouldn't waste any more time on asking.

"Anyway, I miss you," I told her to further smooth my indiscretions over.

"Aww babe. I miss you more."

"You better. Don't be having no niggas over there 'round my girls while I'm gone."

"Boy, stop. He gon' be in here washing dishes by the time you get back. I'ma have that nigga loading up the dishwasher afterwards."

I laughed. "*He* better be yo' muthafuckin' brother, I know that."

"You'll find out when you get here."

"His ass better know how to fight because one thing about me, I don't fuck around."

Iesha laughed. "Whatever babe. You lucky I love your ass."

"Nawl, you the lucky one." I grinned.

"Anyway, I would like to fly out and be there for you when y'all have the funeral. Do you know of any arrangements yet?"

"Yea, the memorial service is very private. We aren't having any public viewings. Right now, only the family knows about it. I believe we're keeping it that way."

"I definitely think that's best, considering the circumstances. Whoever did this was very calculating, and the hatred runs deep for them to do it on the same date as when you lost your parents."

I shook my head. "Tell me about it. They really wanted to hurt us in the worst way, and they succeeded. But when we start our search for answers, it could get real ugly."

"I think you should let the police do their jobs."

"Do you know how many unsolved deaths are in this lil' country ass town alone?"

"No."

"Too fuckin' many. I believe the police are on the thug's payroll that run this shit."

"Hell, I thought James was the thug that ran that shit."

"Yea, me too but, apparently, somebody is bigger than my brother."

"You're right."

"So, I guess you can fly in for the memorial service, but you don't need to stay too long."

"Ok, when is it?"

"Monday morning at ten o'clock."

"Damn, that's early. I ain't never heard of services being that early."

"The earlier the better. Plus, how you were just thinking, everybody else will be thinking the same way."

"My mom will keep the girls."

"Okay good."

"Well, I need to schedule my flight. That's five days from now."

"Yea, so gone do that and call me later. I gotta get my day started."

"Ok babe. Love you."

"Love you too."

"Me and the girls will call on Facetime, so answer the damn phone."

"Can't wait." I grinned, and then she ended the call.

⊰━◈━⊱

Once up, I showered, got dressed and headed downstairs to where I smelled the food coming from.

"I'm glad you stayed here last night," Nana said as she prepared breakfast. "How did you sleep?"

"I slept pretty good. The question is how'd you sleep?" I asked, walking over and kissing her on the cheek.

"If I take them pills the doctor prescribed me, I sleep hard as hell. But if I don't, then I'm up all night. Last night, after all the fun we had, I was up thinking about my babies. Couldn't sleep a wink—"

"Nana, you know you have to take your medicine. For one, it helps keep you relaxed. We don't need nothing happening to you."

"I know, that's why I try to stay busy though."

"I get it, but don't you have a personal chef that cooks around here for y'all?"

"Yea, but I didn't call her in today. I just wanted to cook breakfast for my own family. I'm happy to have you and Remy back home. After all, y'all haven't visited in over ten years."

"But do see y'all at least three times a year. Remember the family gatherings at the cabins or at beach resorts. You love those because all our children get to spend time with each other—"

"Yea, those are my favorite. Now, we'll be missing James and Lovely." She sadly said.

"Nana, I know it's hard but try not to focus so much on that right now," I just felt like the more she dwelled on it, the harder it was going to be for her. "We're gonna have a lot more vacations together, this time the family love will be stronger than before. Yes. Lovely and James are already missed so much, but we have to continue loving on each other even more now."

She wiped the tears from her eyes. "You're right son. You're right."

"Hey Nephew." Maddy smiled, as she joined us.

"Hey Auntie."

"Mama, why you in here cooking? Shan supposed to be taking care of this all week for us."

"I know but I wanted to cook for y'all. I was just telling Joe that I'm glad he and Remy are back home."

"Yea, I'm glad too, but you shouldn't be standing over a stove right now. Did you take your medicine?"

"No, but I'm fine Maddy."

"Mama, I really need you to take care of yourself. I don't know what we'll do—"

"Don't be talkin' like that. I'm grieving my babies. Just let me grieve. I'll be ok. God has me covered."

I shrugged; in that case I guess she was right. So, I'd fall back and let her grieve.

"Good morning family."

"Hey baby," Nana spoke, as Royal made her way around the island stove to kiss her.

"Good morning pretty girl," Auntie spoke.

"Wassup Cuz? Where's my brother?"

"He went back to the hotel after everybody went to bed. He said he'll be back to eat breakfast with us."

"I hope he has reached out to Vanessa by now. That should've been one of the first things he did after getting here," Nana said.

"Mama, the only thing that was on Remy's mind was grieving his sister and his cousin. Plus, Vanessa's got a whole man now."

"Vanessa also got—"

"Mama, chill out. Now ain't the time for that."

I frowned. "Vanessa got what?"

"Nothing," Maddy said with a shake of the head.

"Anyway, set the table Royal. Where is Josette?"

"She was washing bad ass before I came down. She told me to tell you she's coming."

"Don't do my great-nephew." Auntie grinned. "But Lord knows he's bad as hell."

We all laughed.

"I hate to say this but he's gonna be just like his uncle James," Nana teased with a shake of the head. It was good to see her with that loving smile on her face. I don't think I'd seen that look since I got here.

"As much as James played with and deviled him up, I wouldn't be surprised," Auntie added.

"One thing about it, James loved the kids. His children are the same way."

"Speaking of his children, we're having a big family dinner after the service on Monday. I've invited his baby mamas—"

"All three of them country bamma nut cases?" Auntie asked, as I damn near spit my drink out.

"Maddy, be nice. They're family," Nana chimed in.

"No, their kids are family. Not their crazy asses."

"Well, the twins are eleven years old, and they're the oldest. They can't drive themselves here."

"Listen Mama, James has been teaching them boys how to drive for a couple of years now."

I laughed. "He told me he'd started teaching them how to drive."

"The girls too and they ain't but eight, seven and four."

"I'll pick 'em up," Royal chimed in.

Auntie glared at her. "You really wanna pick up that crew? James got some bad ass kids."

We laughed.

"They ain't that bad. Y'all be exaggerating?"

"The boys are getting better with age, but it's the girls now. Every spit of their daddy."

As we laughed and talked about James a lil' more, Remy entered the kitchen. Nana smiled so big, definitely showing that he was her favorite. Rather tickled me but he was the first grand to be born, so I could understand that.

"Good morning family," he said, making his way to Nana and giving her a big fat hug.

Everybody spoke, as I tried to snatch a piece of bacon but got my hand popped in the process.

"Nanaaa," I let out.

"Wait til you eat. You gon' mess up your appetite."

"She ain't changed y'all," Royal laughed.

"What's wrong with you?" I asked Remy, as he sat down at the twelve-chair kitchen table. "You look like you got something on your mind."

"Yea, what's wrong Nephew?"

"Did y'all know that Lovely was pregnant?"

Everybody's eyes stretched.

"Who told you that?" Nana pondered.

"I heard— they say she was pregnant by Rod."

"Rod who?" I asked.

Auntie dropped her head, as if she was disappointed. "Nephew, I know better."

"Rod who?" I asked again with an unsure expression.

"Rodarius Cannon," he answered with a bit of anger in his eyes.

"Nah, that can't be true. Ain't no way Lovely was laying up with the opps."

"Lovely wasn't pregnant. I would've known," Nana said.

"Well, can't you find out? I'm sure somebody knows, the autopsy person— somebody," I responded.

"I still can't believe she was dealing with Rudy's brother. That doesn't make sense," Auntie frowned, just as Josette joined us in the kitchen with her son on her hip.

"Who was dealing with Rudy's brother?" she asked with curious eyes.

"I spoke with someone early this morning who informed me that Lovely was pregnant by Rod."

Josette laughed. "It's a lie. Lovely might've been doing her own thing and lived life like she wanted, but I highly doubt that."

"It's true," Royal softly admitted.

"What?!" Nana shrieked.

"It's true Nana. She'd been fooling around with him for almost two years. I found out a little over a year ago by seeing a text one day while she was doing my hair. She snatched her phone up so quick, but it was too late. I'd already seen the message when it popped up on the display screen. She even had his name saved as Rod C. So, I asked her. She denied it at first, but then she told me the truth. She said they were in love."

"She was in love with the opps?" Remy scowled.

"He wasn't the opps to her and I guess she wasn't the opps to him. It was almost like a forbidden love because they kept that shit a secret for a long time. The timing of it all of it coming out now is puzzling. That's gotta be an inside person talking because nobody knew."

"You didn't tell her no better?." Auntie asked.

"I tried, but you know how Lovely was. She moved at her own melody," Royal stated.

"Wow, this is crazy," I uttered in complete shock.

"I need to sit down. This is too much."

"Yes Mama, please sit down. I'll finish cooking breakfast."

"Don't y'all go out there trying to fight. Please, just stay out of trouble. Y'all boys have changed. I hope this changes Wesley too. Please, don't turn back the time. Y'all have come too far," Nana pleaded.

"Nana, my money too long to mess that up. I'm not doing nothing. Plus, I need more answers than just that," Remy responded. I could tell he didn't want to bad mouth Lovely, none of us did. But it was rather surprising that she would be dating the brother of the nigga that Remy killed some ten years ago.

"Hey everybody," Vanessa waved, as she entered the kitchen out of nowhere.

"What the hell?" Remy uttered, as the rest of us looked with puzzled expressions.

"Vanessa!" Nana called out. "You came just in time. We needed this distraction."

"We did?" Auntie mocked with befuddled eyes.

"Thanks for inviting me to breakfast Nana, but I'm not staying. I just would like a private word with Remy."

"Ohh shit," Auntie uttered.

Remy and Vanessa locked eyes. Just when I thought the morning couldn't get no stranger, it had. Nana didn't give two fucks by hooking this one up and if only I could be a fly on the wall to hear this conversation. *Damn, the real drama was about to begin.*

ISLANDE "REMY" PIERRE

Nessa and I ended up outside on the front patio. She sat down and I followed suit, sitting across from her. I owed this girl a lot and could understand why Nana felt it necessary for us to talk; I just didn't think now was a good time for that. I stared at her, not really knowing what to say. For one, she was even prettier than she was back then. She still had that innocent baby face, bright loving eyes and that laidback lil' casual, plain Jane style of wear. My stomach churned. I hadn't felt this nervous in a long time.

She gazed at me with a quaint smile. "Islande Pierre, it's been a while."

I nodded. "Yea." I responded, just thinking that her and mama were the only two 'round here that ever called me by my government name.

"Let me be more precise. It' been more like ten plus years."

"Yea."

"You look good, Islande."

I nodded. "So do you, Nessa." I wanted to say more but the fucking words just wouldn't come out.

"You ok? I know how much you love your family, and this here is a tough one. I'm still at a loss of words."

"Yea, me too."

"I know we didn't exactly go our separate ways on the best of terms, but I'm truly sorry for your loss. I loved them like they were my own family."

"I know."

She stared at me for a second. I guess she couldn't read my short responses, but I ain't know what to expect. Nessa was too calm and that honestly scared me a little.

"I know how you are, Islande. You're not exactly the type to wear yo' feelings on yo' sleeve. So, but are you really ok? I don't wanna hear you 'round here acting a fool. You hear me? Let the police do their jobs. Somebody will talk."

"Yea, I hear you." I nodded.

"Now, back to me and you." She said, all cool and calm. "Damn, I've missed yo' handsome ass. That jet black slick hair, always trimmed with a fresh tape-up. Those thick, dark eyebrows and light brown eyes that always sucked me in. And now you got the audacity to grow a shallow beard, showing off and shit." She smiled and then, out of nowhere, slapped the shit outta me! I didn't know what happened, but I snapped out of whatever the hell trance I was in.

"What the fuck, Nessa?!"

"I owed yo' ass that shit!" she seethed with a mean glare. Damn, for some reason, that shit took me back to why I loved this woman. She was gangster with it and rode hard for a nigga. She showed me how to love when I'd given up hope. To this day, I'd never met a woman with so much class and gentle nature, yet definitely not the one to be fucked with. If looks could be deceiving was a woman, it would be her. "Where's my fuckin' apology nigga?"

"Damn," I groaned, rubbing the side of my face. "I'm fuckin' sorry."

"Sorry for what?"

"You know what."

"Nawl, I need to hear it. What are you sorry for Islande?"

"Um—"

She caught my ass again, this time with a mean sting to my jaw. "What are you sorry for Islande?"

I just looked at her with a serious stare. I wanted to grab her sexy ass round the neck and fuck the dog shit out her ass, but it was too many people in the house for me to pull that one off.

"Islande?!"

"Ok, I'm sorry for leaving you at the church on our wedding day. Damn, Nessa I'm sorry."

"Do you realize how I've had to live with that day since you left? Nana didn't even know you had changed your flight to leave that same day. Nobody knew that you weren't showing up except you and Joe. I only say Joe because he was with you. You left me, Islande, with no explanation, no excuses, no apology— You wouldn't answer my calls, nothing—"

I regrettably shook my head. "I know and I'm sorry for that. I wasn't ready for marriage. I knew we had talked about it over and over again, but that wasn't it. I needed to get away for me. I couldn't possibly drag you with me. Then, things happened in my life that leveled me so far up, I couldn't look down. That's not to say you're beneath me because I could never think that way about you. I don't think that way about nobody."

"I could never think that you're so high up that you're better than us."

"Because deep down you know me. You've known me longer than any bitch I've ever dealt with. I'm wealthy as fuck but I'm still country as hell. I eat noodles at least twice a week. I still smoke weed and fuck off from time to time. I drive high-priced cars, I wear expensive jewelry, I live in mansions and condos, I vacation in five-star luxury hotels, but none of that can change who the fuck I really am." I explained. "So, please don't think money has changed me. It just changed my environment and the people I deal with on a daily."

"I know that. For one, you didn't have to send me money when you caught that deal. You never said why you sent it, but I took that as an apology that couldn't be said in person. Of course, I wasn't turning that shit down."

"I see you're spending it with a tasteful flare," I smiled, glancing out in the driveway at her white-on-white Range Rover.

"Damn right. If I couldn't get the apology I needed, your money would suffice," she teased with a playful smirk. "Mama appreciates it too. She's now living in her four-bedroom dream home and also driving her dream car—"

"A red Mercedes."

"You remembered."

We laughed.

"How could I forget? She always said, '*when y'all get rich, buy me a red Mercedes and a four-bedroom house. That's all I want.*"

"Who would've known that she had predicted you getting rich?" Nessa grinned.

"I know, right. Hell, I thought I would be living off of dad's settlement money from his software finally jumping off. But, hey, one-million-dollars split between Nana, Natacha, Royal, Lovely and me was nothing—"

"Shit, two-hundred-thousand a piece was a lot of money."

"Not when I was buying jewelry that cost twenty grand plus and driving a luxury car with a pimped-out apartment in New York. The cost of living there is high as fuck. Plus, I'm always gon' be the flyest nigga on the block." I clowned, as she checked out my head-to-toe Gucci attire.

"You ain't telling me nothing I don't know. Your watch probably cost about fifty-thousand."

"Add one-hundred-thousand more to that."

"Oooh, too steep for my taste," she teased. "I can see how you went through that settlement."

"Yea but, the minute that was gone, my own shit popped off."

"I should've been there."

I stared over at her. "You're right. You should've been."

"I wanted to call you and just say congratulations but by, then it, was apparent that what we had was long over. The only thing I kept thinking was how the hell you managed to come out with a fuckin' dating app looking for love, yet you left me at the altar. You hurt me," she declared with glossy eyes.

"I know."

"So, you got a woman? In a serious relationship?"

I frowned. "Hell nawl. These bitches just wanna have my baby."

She laughed. "Arrogant ass."

"Ain't nothing changed." I grinned. "You got a nigga?"

"Um—"

"That's either yeah or no."

"Why? That ain't ya business Mr. Pierre."

I shrugged. "Okay, if you say so."

"I just have to be careful, ya know. Some niggas just wanna live off a bitch."

I grinned. "If that nigga don't work he a fuckin' leach. You too bad on all levels to be fuckin' 'round like that. But hey, I can hold it down for ya if need be while I'm on this end."

She laughed. "You wish."

"Can you grant me a couple of 'em? Promise to use 'em—"

Quickly, she intervened. "Ain't nobody hittin' this, includin' you."

"Yeah right. Somebody beatin' that pussy. If not, it's some lame ass niggas round here."

"Hush boy," she grinned. "I'm just doing me, whatever that consist of. If it is a nigga gettin' a taste of this, you won't know."

"Ok." I coolly shrugged.

"Anywayssss, moving on. Wassup with Natacha? Have you heard from her?"

"No," I responded. "Nana called, no answer. They stopped by her place; she wasn't there."

"I know she's heard about Lovely and James and for her that's gotta be devastating as fuck. Don't you think?"

I shrugged. "I would think so, but we don't really keep in contact with each other. She has chosen to live by her lonesome for over twenty-three years. Who am I to interfere with that?"

"Somebody should really keep trying to locate her, though," she suggested.

"If she wants to be found, she'll come out of hiding."

"Okaaay," Nessa sang, then changed the subject. "So, how's Wesley?"

"He's ok. I'm going by his crib when I leave here. You know Gaelle ain't letting him out her eyesight."

Nessa laughed. "I know, right. They're so cute together. Every time I see them, I think that could've been us."

"Hm," I sighed. Taking a ride down memory lane wasn't what I needed at the moment. But damn, just being in her presence took me there.

"But, hey. I won't go there. I've let it go and moved on." She confessed and then changed the subject. "I hate talking about this too, but have you heard anything yet? The streets aren't really talking."

"Nothing," I responded.

I really didn't want to tell her that I'd heard Lovely was pregnant by the opps. Only because I didn't know what that was about. Everybody knew how deep the beef was between us and the Cannons. Rod was the brother right under Rudy. I didn't discriminate against which brother I hated the most. Somewhere in the scheme of things I ended up fucking two of Rod's bitches, he tried fuckin' mine but couldn't succeed. I had Nessa on lock. Nevertheless, the fights seemed to always start with James and Tony, the youngest Cannon brother.

Then, one day, me and Rudy locked in at a fuckin' cookout a mutual associate was throwing. In front of everybody there, I knocked his ass into a deep sleep. Had him laid out in the front yard snoring. The beef was squashed then and there. So, who would've thought that almost two years later, I'd be facing murder charges for killing him? Some said they saw it coming. Even more said he had it coming. Either way, my heart was pretty cold back then, which was why I knew I needed to leave here. Now that cold heart was back.

"Why is the police coming here?"

I glanced out, scouring the twenty acres of land to see that there was a cop car making its way up the pathway to Nana's house.

"Why they coming here?" Nessa repeated.

I shrugged. "I don't know. Probably to pay their respects. It ain't like Nana ain't known around here."

"Yea, probably," Nessa responded as she curiously stared at me.

"What?"

She shook her head. "Nothing."

"It's something. I haven't forgotten that look."

"I'm just thinkin'. You're a changed man Islande. Don't—"

"Don't what, you don't want me to turn into the nigga you used to know?" I pondered with serious eyes.

"Yea, you're better than this. You got too much to lose. I know you loved James and Lovely but—" She paused as the cop car parked, and two officers stepped out. "We'll talk about this later," she said, "Is that Gene?"

"Damn, he still on the force?"

"Yea, he's a detective now. He don't usually ride around in police cars, though."

"Well, he did get out on the passenger side," I commented, as they made their way up to the enclosed porch. I stood up and walked out in the yard to greet them. Nessa was right behind me like the lil' rider I remembered her to be.

"Wassup Remy?" Gene coolly asked, holding his hand out to shake mine. "Long time no see."

"Wassup Gene. I see you're still policing the city," I teased, shaking his hand.

"Actually, I'm a detective now."

"So, I've heard," I coolly nodded. "Officerrr— Smith?" I said, quickly having read his name tag.

"Yea, I've heard a lot about you."

"Oh, have you? Well, you know what they say. The old me doesn't live here no more."

"Hey Gene— Smith," Nessa said. It was no surprise she knew them. In this city, it felt like everybody knew everybody, at least in this neck of the woods.

"Hey Vanessa," Gene spoke back.

"Nessa," Officer Smith smiled, as I frowned a bit.

"So, what brings y'all out in the country?" I asked.

"Well, first, we wanna give our condolences to and the family. I'm sorry to hear about your family. Just know we're doing everything possible to find out who's responsible for this."

"It's been three days Gene. Y'all still don't have any leads?"

"We do."

"So, what's taking so long?"

"Islande—" Nessa intervened. "Is there a reason y'all are here other than paying your respects?"

"Well, um—" Officer Smith started, but Gene cut in.

"Stoney Harris was killed last night."

"And who is that?" I asked.

"A neighborhood wanna-be thug," Nessa uttered.

"He's someone who had known issues with your cousin James."

"Ok, and you're telling me this because?"

"Because I need to know where you were last night," Gene said.

"He was here," Nana responded out of nowhere. "Are you seriously here questioning my grandson after we've just lost two of our own?"

"Uh—hi Mrs. Pierre. I'm sorry for your loss."

"Save it Gene," she immediately sassed.

"I'm just doing my job, Mrs. Pierre. I heard Joe and Remy were back in town and considering their past, I had to come out and question them."

"You didn't have to do nothing because what you need to be doing is finding out who the hell killed my babies. That's yo' fuckin' job! Yet, here you are way out here in the country asking them questions about somebody that neither of my boys knew."

"You sure?" Officer Smith asked.

"Gene, get yo' do-boy befo—"

"Aye, Remy—" Joe called out, grabbing me by the arm.

"Do-boy?" Officer Smith glared.

"I don't stutter nigga. Fuckin' badge don't scare me. Do you know who the hell—"

"No, unt-unt. Nephew, let's go in the house." Maddy stepped in.

"Y'all should be ashamed," Nessa fussed with an irritated shake of the head. "They're grieving and this what y'all do?"

"Nessa, you know we just doing our jobs, right?" Officer Smith explained, as Nessa held her hand up in his face.

"This ain't it Darnell."

"Come on Nessa!" I called out. "Fuck these petty ass cops."

"Get off my property," Nana told 'em.

I hated cussing like that in front of Nana, but I'd lost my cool. How dare these niggas show up to question us about a murder when they ain't even figured out who killed Lovely and James yet? The fuckin' audacity of it all was mind blowing.

"Remy, calm down," Nana said as she rubbed me on the back. "Just calm down."

"I'm calm."

"If that's calm, I'd hate to see what angry is," Royal blurted.

"Who is that rookie cop?"

Everybody looked at Nessa.

I frowned. "That's yo' man or something?"

"Well—"

"Rent a cop yo' nigga?" I asked again, but this time in a high-pitched tone.

"Yea, and—" she answered with an unbothered expression on her face.

I brushed it off like it was nothing, but now I was really wishing I would've laid his ass out. "Well, check him before I do." I said in a serious tone. "You must not have told him about me."

"Why would I? It's embarrassing enough the whole town knows how you did me?"

"That was ten years ago. Get over it lady," I griped.

"Get over it? Did you just tell me to get over it?! Nigga, I will smack the fire out yo' ass—"

"And I'll smack the fire out yo' nigga ass—"

"Do it and watch yo' ass be in handcuffs."

"You think I care 'bout that? I'll bond out before he can get me in his car!"

"You one lame ass nigga."

I shot her ass the dirtiest look I could muster up. "Nessa, keep running off at the mouth and watch I fuck yo' nigga up!"

Josette quickly intervened, "Aye, y'all chill out. Nana already got enough on her plate."

"You're right Josette." Nessa coolly nodded. "I'm leaving."

"Don't forget to tell yo' lil' rent a cop boyfriend 'bout me."

Nessa shot me the middle finger. "Forget you, Islande. Even with all the money in the world, he's still more man than you," she seethed. "Sorry 'bout this y'all."

"Damn," Joe uttered, as I shot his ass an irritated look.

"Let's ride," I told him.

"Don't go out there messing with that girl!" Nana called out.

"I ain't sayin' nothing to her. We going to Wesley's."

***

After ten minutes of silence, I looked over at Joe, who was staring out the window and bobbing his head to the music. "Can you believe what just happened?"

"Nawl, Gene still be with the bullshit, I see."

"Nigga couldn't hardly speak and show his condolences without the look of jealousy written all over his face."

"I peeped that shit when we walked outside," Joe said as he looked in the rearview mirror. "Have you noticed that car following us?"

"Hell yea. I was about to ask you the same thing."

"We've been gone so long, we don't even know vehicles 'round this bitch."

"I know. Get the gun out the glove box."

"Shit, I got mine on me but here." He pulled out my Glock, handing it to me. I sat it in my lap, watching the road and the car behind us.

"These lil' niggas round here gon' learn today."

"Yeah, they probably think since bro gone and Wesley laid up, they can turn up on us but ain't nothing. Either they forgot or a nigga ain't told 'em no better."

"Yeah, well, Ion like how close this car is ridin' on my bumper."

"Pull over and see what they do."

"You're right." I eased over on the side of the road. The car shot by me, blowing the horn. "You recognize them niggas?"

"Nawl, but it's a car full of 'em."

"I see." The car slowed down in front of us and then a hand flew out the window. He was pointing towards the store. "Listen, if these niggas want some smoke, I'm ready to give it to 'em."

"Say less. Follow 'em."

We pulled into the store's parking lot right behind the blue tricked-out Cutlass. "They gotta be jits still rolling on twenty-eights."

Joe laughed. "It's a country thang. Don't act like you forgot."

I grinned. "Oh, I remember. That indigo blue hittin' too."

"Hell yeah," Joe agreed.

I parked, as a Lil' nigga with free form wicks in his head and a mouth full of gold jumped out the car. He was grinning from ear to ear. I opened my door with my piece in my hand. I had a billion dollars ridin' on me deadin' his lil' ass right here in the parking lot if he got outta line.

"Woooah." He backed up with his hands in the air. "You'n need that fam."

"Who you?" I asked, as Joe crept up behind him, his hand over his piece that was tucked in the front of his jeans.

"Ayyye, it's me. Nicholas. Remember Lil' Nico," he acknowledged as his homies climbed out the car.

"Wesley's lil' cousin?" Joe asked.

"Yeah, that's me." He cheesed.

"Damn, Nico." I grinned, now putting my piece away. "Nigga, you grown now. You was 'round twelve, thirteen years old when we left. I should've known who you were. You and Wesley favor with those wicks in y'all hair."

"Hell yeah. That's comes from our Haitian side." He grinned. "Ayee y'all, this Remy and Joe. They're Wesley's cousins on his mama side. This the nigga that smoked Rudy."

"Oooooh shit, you're a legend 'round here my nigga!" one of the other boys yelled.

The other four niggas crowded 'round us. Everybody wanted dap, as Joe stood there smiling. He loved this shit. I was sure it took him back to his bodyguard days. Seriously, all of us were the muscle, but we were clear on our roles.

"Aye, we just wanna say we're sorry to hear 'bout James and Lovely. That was fucked up. We did a lot of work for James. That nigga took care of us," Nico explained.

"He sholl did," another nigga chimed in.

"That's wassup fam. Have y'all heard anything? Do y'all know who would've done this to them?" Joe asked.

"James was a real one and that made him a lot of enemies. We don't know who could've been that bold to do some foul shit like that. I mean, the nigga practically ran the city."

"I know." Joe nodded with a serious face.

"When y'all left, James and Wesley took over. They stood up to any nigga that looked at 'em funny. Wesley was cooler, whereas James was the real crazy one. You couldn't underestimate either though. About a month ago, James pistol-whipped Stoney for not paying him his money."

I frowned. "Talkin' 'bout that nigga who got killed last night?"

"Hell yeah," Nico responded.

"So, y'all think he had something to do with it?"

"Hell nawl," one of the niggas let out. "That nigga was on drugs. That's why James had to fuck him up. Plus, he ain't got no heart like that. He ain't got no pull like that either. It wasn't him."

"Well, who killed him?" I pondered.

"Shit, we don't know," Nico answered.

"So, now, it's three murders in less than three days and nobody knows nothing?" Joe asked.

Nico simply shook his head. "Nobody." He shrugged. "How long y'all in town?"

"Until we find out what happened."

"Do you know how many unsolved deaths this city got? Y'all might be here for a while."

"Even if the police don't find out, we will," I assured him. "What y'all niggas 'bout to do?"

"Head over here to Lil' Chick and set up shop. That's where we be hanging out at. We got the owner on payroll. Hopefully, we can keep it that way since James gone. But, thankfully, Wesley still here. I'm gone miss James though. We all are."

I nodded, definitely agreeing with that part.

"Where y'all headed at?"

"Wesley's," I answered.

"Tell that nigga to holla at me. I talked to him the other day, but Ion wanna keep bothering him right now. Just tell him if he got anything he need us to do and I mean anything, to holla at us."

"A'ight."

"Good to see y'all man. Y'all niggas looking good. Looking like money!" Nico cheesed. "By the way, I love that car. Is it bulletproof?"

"Shoot at it and find out." I smirked.

"Oh shit! You can tell where the money at!" Nico shrieked, giving his homey dap. "Aye, if y'all need anything while y'all in town, don't hesitate to hit my line. We got you! Whatever it is!"

"Preciate that fam," Joe said, giving him dap.

I gave 'em dap. "We'll see y'all around." I nodded. We got in the car. As I backed out the store's parking lot, thoughts surfaced as to what really could've happened that night. Something was going on and whatever it was had to be intense as fuck. I didn't know all the ends and outs of what was happening with my family. I just knew they were deep in the streets, but this shit must be solved and we didn't care how that had to happen.

WESLEY "WES" PIERRE

The past three days damn near seemed like a blur. Losing my cousins happened so fast, it was almost hard for me to remember it. I'd tried replaying the moment in my mind more than a few times, just wanting to revisit some kind of clues as to who could've done this to us. I knew without a doubt that it was more than one person, that part was for sure. The car itself was riddled with over forty shots. Most of those were targeted at Lovely and James, who were in the front seat. That's how I somehow made it out alive. Of course, I'd had my niggas in the streets still reporting back to me with theories or what they assumed, but nobody had any solid leads. As I laid on my stomach watching *Scarface* and scrolling through IG, my cell phone rang. I glanced down to see that it was Madeline Pierre. Quickly, I answered.

"Wassup mom?"

"Hey son, what you doing?"

"Just staying off my ass," I joked. "I mean, literally."

She grinned. "Gettin' shot twice in the ass ain't no joke, huh?"

"Hell nawl. Shit aggy, man, but I'm gettin' better."

"Every time I hear your voice, I thank God you're still here," she said through a choked tone.

"Ma, don't start that crying. I'm tryna be strong here. We ain't even laid 'em to rest yet, and I already know we gon' need a registered nurse on stand-by. Plus, for now, I gotta keep my head on straight."

"I know, son. It's just hard to believe they're gone. I find myself waiting up for Lovely to come home. You know she was always the one that stayed out later than everybody else. Sometimes not coming home for days, but she'd still call. I still heard her voice every day."

"I know, ma."

"Mama still taking it hard, but she'll get through it. She's dealt with loss before. Maybe not on this scale, but she's a survivor. I wish you would just come here until you heal up. At least she'd get to see you."

"You know how Gaelle is. She wants me here with her."

"Hell, Gaelle can bring her lil' skinny ass over here too."

"She would, but you know her and Josette don't exactly like each other."

"Ain't nobody stun that shit right now. This house big as hell for a reason. They don't even have to see each other. Mama still wants all y'all here. Plus, we're grieving. Josette lost a brother and a cousin. She ain't thinking about Gaelle. I know Gaelle isn't to blame for their lil' feud, but you know Josette. She's a mean one."

"Tell me about it. I think she be mean muggin' me because me and Gaelle got back together. But that's my girl. She gon' always be my girl. We went through some crazy shit back then. I knew why she left me and did what she did—"

"You was a hoe, just admit it."

"That's what I'm saying, lady."

Mama laughed. "Anyway, Gaelle can't expect to be a part of the family if she don't wanna be around us."

"Maaaa, I get it," I groaned. "I'll talk to her. I believe she knows how important it is for us to be around each other. So, we'll come over tomorrow and stay until after the memorial service. You satisfied?"

"Yes and thank you. So, what you doing?"

"Laying here scrolling IG," I repeated, like she hadn't already asked that question.

"Where's Gaelle, anyway?"

"Grilling me a sandwich."

"I was coming over today but, since you're coming here tomorrow, I'll wait."

"You still could've came."

"Remy and Joe are on the way over. I know how it is when y'all get together. They should be there shortly."

"Oh, good. I can't wait to see 'em."

"So, guess what happened earlier?"

"What?"

"Nessa came over."

My eyes stretched open. "Oh shit. Was Remy there?"

"Yep."

"Ooooh, Nana so messy. I already know she set that up." I grinned.

"You definitely know yo' grandmother," she laughed.

"Did they fight? You know that woman is borderline crazy. That's why they made such a good couple. They were time enough for each other."

"Like you can talk. You and Gaelle the same way."

I laughed. "And is. That's why we make a good couple, too."

"Boy hush," she teased and continued. "A[...]
Remy and Nessa ended up going outside to talk. I can't [...]
what happened while they were out there but, knowin[...]
Nessa, she probably did swing on him."

I laughed. "If she did, who could blame her?"

"I do know that after Gene and Officer Smith left here, they got into an argument."

"Hol' up, huh?"

"I said, after Gene—"

"No, I mean, why were the police there?"

"Oh yeah, guess I should've started with that first huh?"

"Right but, with you, gossip always takes precedence over important shit," I teased.

"Boy hush," she sassed. "Anyway, they came out here to question Joe and Remy. Apparently, some dude that James had beef with got killed last night. They needed to make sure that they didn't have nothing to do with it."

"So, this nigga Gene drove way out there in the country questioning them when he ain't even found out who killed our peeps?"

"Well, you know Mama snapped on his ass."

"She should've."

"We had to damn near drag Remy in the house because I just knew he was 'bout to fight 'em."

"Remy and Gene 'bout to fight?"

"You know Remy's mouth. Shit took me back to how he used to be. Thank God time has changed him a little, or they asses would've been napping in Mama's front yard."

e been there."

hurt ass was gon' do?"

ı niggas on Nana's twenty acres of land."

ghed out loud.

¬Stop playing around, lady. I ain't that hurt. When I get on these Percs and weed, Ion feel shit."

She laughed. "High ass. Anyway, let me finish boy. Shit was already weird enough with Nessa and Darnell being in the same space as Remy—"

"Oh shit, I forgot they messin' around."

"Exactly!"

"So, what happened?"

"I think Remy was already putting the two together, just because Darnell kept calling her Nessa and, then, she even called him by his name. But he got smart with Mama and that put the icing on the cake."

"Damn. It really went that far?"

"Yeah, but the real shit hit the fan when they left. That's when him and Nessa exchanged words. To a point that Josette had to step in to calm them down because baby, Mama wasn't sayin' nothing. It was almost like her name was Wes and she wasn't in that mess."

I laughed out loud. "Damn, I missed the drama."

"You did. I know yo' ass would've enjoyed that. I think we all needed that lil' distraction, even though the shit was bogus on Gene's part. He knew better than showing up like that."

"My thoughts exactly."

"Anyway, I really wanna know if you knew anything about that boy that got killed last night?"

"Nawl."

"So, you didn't even hear about it?"

"Nawl."

"Yeah right. I know yo' ass. You too deep in the streets to have not heard. So, you didn't?"

"Nawl."

"Son—"

"Mama, I ain't have nothing to do with it, okay. Stop questioning me like you the damn police."

"Boy, I can ask you whatever the hell I wanna ask you."

"Okay, you got that," I responded, just as Gaelle entered the bedroom.

"Got your grilled ham and cheese sandwich bae."

"Thanks bae. You gon' feed it to me?"

"Boy." she smiled. "I guess since you can't sit on yo' ass. Who you talking to?"

"Mama."

"Oh."

"That's all she gotta say?"

I shook my head. Madeline Pierre was always fuckin' extra, but I had something for her ass. "Mama said hey with yo' pretty tail self."

"Tell her heyyy." Gaelle smiled.

"She is pretty, but I didn't say shit. She was supposed to speak to me first."

"Lady, lemme call you back." I grinned, ending the call. "Mama wants us to come stay to the house till after the service."

"You know Josette don't care for me, and I ain't got time for her shit."

"You and Josette need to get over that old shit. If I ain't trippin' 'bout it, then nobody should be trippin' 'bout it."

"Tell ya cousin that with her big ole booty, crazy tail self."

I grinned. "Don't hate on my cousin's booty because yours flat."

"It won't be after I have my surgery next week. This ass gon' be fat baby."

I smiled. "And I can't wait. I'm gon' be hittin' that thang from the back all the time. Leavin' my handprint on it, smacking that fat ass," I teased with a devious grin. "Just watch and see."

"You so damn nasty," she laughed. Her tone always tickled me. Before NuNu on ATL, there was Gaelle with that country ass, sexy accent.

We laughed, just as the doorbell rang.

"That's Remy and Joe. Let 'em in."

"Okay— well, I'm gon' go 'head and run my errands since you'll have yo' peeps here to watch your hurt booty ass. Love you." Gaelle kissed me with a soft chuckle.

"A'ight, we gon' see whose booty hurtin' when I drink some liquor on these Percs and fuck the shit outta yours," I laughed. "Dooty-hole sore the next day."

"Boy please, one pump and yo' ass gon' be hollin'."

I bust out laughing. "That's a'ight. If that don't work, I'm gon' shoot you in the ass. Keep playin'."

Gaelle bust out laughing as she exited the room. "Boy please!"

I could hear her greeting Joe and Remy as they came into the house. "He's in the entertainment room. It's great to see y'all. I'm just sorry that it's under these circumstances," she said. They had a lil' small talk and, minutes later, Joe entered the room first.

"Nigga, how that ass feel?!"

"Loudmouth ass boy. Don't start that shit." I playfully mugged.

Joe laughed while sitting down. "Damn nigga, you still love this movie?"

"Hell yeah. I watch it at least once a week."

"I bet you do," Remy chimed in as he joined us. "We always knew you were gon' be a knucklehead. The only way to quiet yo' hyper ass down when we were younger was to pop in this movie."

"Damn right. Scarface is my muthafuckin' idol."

"Like we don't know that," Joe clowned. "Anyway, nigga, did you do it?"

"Do what?"

"Did you have that lil' nigga knocked off. The one that James had beef with?"

"Yeah, did you do it? Did you cover yo' tracks? Do I need to make sure this shit don't come back to you?" Remy pondered all in one breath.

I frowned. "Listen, y'all sound like yo' nosey ass auntie."

"Shit, we just askin'. We know how you get down," Joe added. "We already met lil' Nico at the store with his goons. Of course, they weren't talking."

"Actin' clueless and shit," Remy uttered. "And Nico looking just like yo' ass with that crazy looking hair."

I grinned while shaking my head. "Lay off the hair, my nigga. Anyway, listen, that feud between James and Stoney wasn't shit. The lil' nigga grew some balls and tried James. Blame it on the coke because a bitch knows better. He was geeked and felt froggy, so he jumped outta pocket and took a package with no intent to pay for it. But after that ass cuttin' James put on him, he sobered the fuck up. It was just too late, though. The damage was done," I explained. "So, to answer yo' question, I really didn't have nothing to do with that. He must've pissed somebody else off too. It wouldn't be surprising."

"So, you don't think he was in on the shit? I mean, after all, James had whooped his ass and everybody knew about it. He could've been big mad enough to go out and set that shit up."

"Nah, that nigga ain't retaliating. He wouldn't even have the back to support him. Whoever did this shit had the muscle. It's only a couple of niggas 'round here that I think would try us—"

"Who is that?" Remy asked.

"The Cannons, Duck and Busy."

"Who the fuck is Duck and Busy?"

"Two brothers from 'round the way with that bag. We used to serve 'em until they linked with somebody else. After that, the niggas started acting funny towards us. Shit, Duck and James even exchanged words at 'Lil Chick one day. Shit would've gone way left had Gene not pulled up. After that, it was definitely some apparent smoke in the air. We don't even serve like we used to, but we're known to have quality over quantity and niggas like Duck and Busy be hatin' on that shit. For us, that's just play money. That's how we keep niggas on payroll and ready for war if necessary. We could've been ran them niggas outta town but ain't nobody 'round here fuckin' with us on no level. We got the real bag."

"Damn right." Remy nodded.

"So, wassup with the Cannons? That's old beef, but I'm sure it's still brewing. Which brings me to question this shit Remy heard about Lovely. Was she really fuckin' Rod?" Joe pondered.

I looked over at Remy. "Remember the night when it happened? I was trying to tell you before she ended the call with you. She kept telling me to hush, though."

"I remember. So, how you knew?"

"She told me."

"So, James knew too?"

"Hell nawl."

"I was 'bout to say." Remy mugged.

"Me and Lovely were real tight. We talked about shit that she could never tell James. Y'all know James was a fool. They didn't call him *that crazy Baptiste boy* for nothing."

"Shit, they called Remy *that crazy Pierre boy* too."

"Why you think they were the tightest two?" I chuckled. "Birds of a muthafuckin' feather—"

"Aye, hol' up; leave my brother outta this. He ain't here to defend himself."

"Nigga, dem apples didn't fall too far from the tree. You in this shit too."

"Right."

Joe laughed. "Whatever niggas."

"Anyway, James wouldn't have went for that. He probably would've choked the shit outta Lovely."

"I can see that happening." Remy nodded. "So, do you think Rod had something to do with it? After all, I was told she was pregnant. Maybe things were good as long as they were lowkey but bringing a baby in the world is next level."

"I didn't know that. She kept that part a secret if she was. She just acted like her, and the nigga had broken up. I figured she was lyin' though. She really liked that nigga. But who tellin' you this shit? I mean, about her being pregnant? Miss Martha, ain't it?"

"Hell yeah." Remy nodded. "You know I couldn't stop til I paid her a visit earlier this morning."

Martha was the town's psychic. She was always in somebody's business and knew what was going to happen before it happened. She and Nana were once best of friends way, way back when— until word around town said that Martha and granddaddy were messing around. At least that's what Nana told us, and she didn't mind adding '*y'all get your hoe 'ish ass ways from your granddaddy. God rest his soul*'."

I sighed. "Martha is usually right about a lot of things," I said. "But for her to call his name and give that exact information, a very reliable source told her."

"That's true because she don't ever call out names. She'll point in that direction, but nawl— however, Royal confirmed it. We're just waiting on the autopsy to tell us more."

"So, Royal knew too?" I pondered. "Hm, well it had to be true. What else did Martha say?"

"That the people aren't from around here. Don't mean they don't live here, but they definitely aren't from Gainesboro."

"Interesting," I uttered. "Anything else?"

"She kept saying that she sees the color blue but, then, she said gray. It could mean a boy, the sky." Remy shrugged. "Hell, could be the colors someone is wearing, um—who knows? You know some of those readings can be vague as hell and it don't fully come together until it comes together."

"Right." Joe nodded.

"So, if she's sayin' that they're not from around here, then it can't be the Cannons, but Busy and Duck moved here from Florida."

"Interesting," Joe said.

"I would hate to think it's them, but let's face it. They couldn't stand us, especially James. It would also be in their best interest to get rid of the competition. They could've easily recruited some niggas that weren't from this area to do the dirty work. I mean, nobody knows of that car. Last I was told, the video image was somewhat grainy, but they could make out the car being a Beretta. It was also three people with ski masks on that was shooting. One even stepped out the car. That's the one that caught James."

"A fuckin' Beretta? Who the hell still driving that old shit?"

"Exactly," Joe eased in.

"Can't be nobody from 'round here. Whoever that was used that car strictly for what they had planned that night."

"Damn, I still can't believe it. It just seems so surreal to be here after ten years, but also to know that we won't be seeing them. I'm still so in disbelief, I don't know what to do. We can't retaliate right now if we wanted to. That's what they're expecting us to do. You know, sometimes, you make a name that never leaves you. People in this city still look at us as the town's bullies. The crazy niggas. You and James hadn't made it no better over the years—"

"Shit, we wasn't as crunk as we were back in the day though. We calmed down a lot. We have niggas on payroll to do our dirty work and they'll take the charge for it if necessary. Trust me, we've come too far and our money is too long to get caught up in some crazy shit."

"Good." Remy nodded. "I'll be talking to Santana Saturday morning when he makes it here. This is one case that won't go unsolved. The people that did this to Lovely and James gon' pay for it. I can promise you that."

"If anybody can get to the bottom of this, it'll be Santana," Joe said. "I wanted to ask about him. But I know he lost his grandmother a couple of weeks ago and has been dealing with that. So, after you never mentioned him, I figured that's why."

"Yeah, I wasn't gon' bother him because I can only imagine what losing her was like, but he called and insisted that he get on this. He is the best P.I. I know."

"Well, make sure you get with Gene, so you can find out as much as possible about this case. That way, Santana will have all the information he needs to get started."

"Man, fuck Gene. He still got some kind of ill feelings against me. They should never hire clown ass niggas that was a joke in school to work on the force. Them be the ones that act off emotion and be thinking their badge will save 'em. Fuck a badge. I'll still knock his square ass off the map," Remy stated.

"After you left, we ain't have no issues outta Gene. I believe it was just you he was happy to be rid of."

"Let's face it. You fucked his girl in high school. You fucked his other bitch after he became a police—"

"And let's not forget you fucked his sister too, because the nigga pulled you over and gave you a fuckin' speedin' ticket," I laughed. "You a cold ass muthafucka. For somebody to have created a dating app I would think you'd be more of a lover, but shiiitt. You're more of a heartbreaker."

"Man, that was a long time ago. I done changed."

"Have you?" I asked. You ain't had a steady woman since you been gone."

"That's a lie. Me and Regan—"

Joe laughed out loud. "Regan breaks up with you every other week."

"Oh, y'all niggas got jokes huh? Fuck y'all, fuck Gene and fuck his lil' rent a cop side-kick."

Me and Joe bust out laughing.

"Oh, you know Mama told me what happened. Gene was dead ass wrong for that shit. He knows it. But how you feel about ya girl and Darnell talking?"

Remy shrugged. "Should I have feelings about that? I mean, I don't."

"And you wonder why we call you cold."

"Whatever. The only feelings I have is leaving her at the church that day. That lil' nigga she fuckin' ain't on my level. He really ain't got shit to offer her. She just doing something to past the time by."

They laughed.

"Shit ain't funny." I grinned, with a regrettable shake of the head. "Damn, I believe I fucked up, though.

Looking at her fine ass now, I wished I would've locked her in back then."

"Really cuz?" I grinned.

"Shit, have you seen her?" he asked in a high-pitched tone.

"Hell yeah, I see her around all the time. Nana always inviting her to the house. I believe that's Nana's way of staying close to you. I know it sounds funny, but you and Nessa had been fooling around since y'all were 'bout eleven years old."

"She was that one best friend I had when I lost dad and auntie," he said while looking in Joe's direction. I could tell he didn't wanna bring up that conversation, so he moved on. "I can't lie, I still love that girl. I know she's moved on but that don't mean we can't be cordial. However, she did slap the shit outta me—"

"I knew it!" I shouted with laughter. "Nessa wasn't gon' let you slide embarrassing her like that. Hell, I don't blame her."

"I know man. I don't even wanna think about it. Sending her a big ass check won't make up for the shit I did, but I still owe her. I'll always owe her."

"Well, you know she owns The Spotlight."

"James told me a lil' bit 'bout it some months back?"

"It's going out towards highway 80," I informed him. "It's nice as fuck. We should hit that bitch up Saturday night."

"Nigga, how you going somewhere and you can't even sit on yo' ass?" Remy asked, as Joe kee-kee'd.

"That's three days away. Shit, I'll be better than good by then."

"We might have to turn that bitch out if muthafuckas think it's sweet over this way," Joe chimed in.

"I was just thinking that. You know how niggas will try you just to prove a point. Ya lil' gang gang said I was a legend 'round here. Somebody might wanna try to dethrone my ass."

"Yeah, well, you'll be the last nigga they'll ever think about fuckin' with. I put that shit on fam," I said.

"Shit, I say let's do it. I ain't been out in Gainesboro in a long time. I know it's gon' feel different without James somewhere gettin' fucked up and grabbing ass—"

"And Lovely at the bar beatin' a bitch outta money to buy her a drink."

We laughed.

"But it's gon' be one helluva night and I'm looking forward to it," I added with a smile. Saturday couldn't get here fast enough.

ISLANDE "REMY" PIERRE

I sat at the desk inside of my hotel suite, writing out a twenty-thousand-dollar check to give to one of the best private-eye detectives around.

"Santana! My guy!" I smiled, handing over the check.

"Boy, you know I'd do this shit for nothing, right?"

"I know but you're taking this money. I can't just let you work a case and don't pay you for it. That's unethical, friends or not."

"Yeah, but we more like partners. I scratch your back, you scratch mine."

"But this here is the biggest scratch I've ever needed. Somebody took the life of my people and I need answers. I'm trying not to revert back to my old ways. By now, I'd be in the streets asking questions, laying niggas out, pistol whipping a bitch, all that. But I can't be moving like that no more. I refuse to be another statistic or a nigga that made it out but ended up back in."

"I'm glad you're thinking this through because all week, I was preparing myself to either bail you out of jail or fly here to Georgia guns blazing."

I chuckled. "Hell yeah. I often think you're a long-lost brother that my parents didn't tell us about."

We laughed.

"Could be," Santana agreed. "So, how are you holding up?"

"I'm good bro. I won't know how it'll be when I see them but, for now, I'm good."

"So, you never went to see 'em?"

"Nawl, I believe that would've been more than I could handle. I mean, I'm already trying not to snap on these bitch ass niggas 'round here. Seeing them like that would've only intensified my desire to get to the bottom of things on my own. Let's just say that wouldn't have been good for nobody, including myself."

"You're right. So, how's Joe? I know this gotta be tough for him."

"Yeah, it is, but you know Joe. He deals with things a lot differently than me. I wouldn't even know what he's thinking if I don't ask. He's pretty chill about his feelings. I know he's had his moments when he's alone but, once he emerges, he's back to ole, cool ass Joe."

"Damn, I feel bad for my boy, though."

"You and me both. Him and James were always so opposite. Joe was more of the nonchalant one that could easily fool a nigga that ain't know any better. Don't get it twisted, and you're even a witness to this. He has always been just as wild and foolish as the rest of us. He's just laid back with it."

"Oh, I know. Since this happened, has he spoken about his parents? It's just crazy that the shit happened on the twenty-third anniversary of them dying."

I looked at Santana with a shake of the head. "Now, you know better. I know it's not easy for him to talk to me about that situation. After all, his father killed my dad, my auntie and then killed himself all while him, Josette and James were in the house. James and Joe were the ones that came outside to see them laid out in the yard like that, and Joe called for help. That not only was the worst day of their life but mine too. Hell, my whole family for that matter," I said, sipping from my glass of Deleon Tequila. "That shit devastated us all, especially my mom. She and Aunt Nadia were twins. She lost half of herself and never was the same, while giving birth to Royal the day after. Then, months later, she started using drugs to deal with the pain of it all and simply wasn't there for us like she should've been. Several times, in between her back-and-forth stages, she attempted suicide, but God wasn't ready for her. Nana mentioned that she once told her she was in a better place of not loving anybody. So, if she could stay away long enough, she'd learn to unlove us," I revealed, almost getting choked up. I had never spoke about this but, for some reason, I needed to get it off my heart.

"Damn, that's deep Bro."

"I know. For a long time, I had no desires to see her. I felt like she left us at a time when we really needed her."

"Yeah, but you gotta understand where she was coming from. I'm not saying that she was right, but some people deal with things a whole lot differently than others. She lost a whole twin and her husband. Didn't you say when they got married, he took her last name instead of her taking his?"

"Yeah."

"Hell, that tells you how much he loved her. So, for her to lose a man that loved her that deeply and her twin sister was major. She was broken beyond repair at that time. What she needed was for everybody to rally around her."

"We tried but we were just kids. I was ten years old when that happened. Nana was dealing with losing a daughter and two son-n-laws. Aunt Maddy was dealing with losing a sister and two brother-n-laws. We have other family members, but they weren't in our immediate circle. So, after having Royal, I guess it just became too much—"

"Which could explain why she was mentally unprepared for the battle that was ahead. She could've not only been grieving but dealing with post-partum and all that. You can't keep looking at her like she's the bad guy.

What she needs is love, not space. Everybody, and I'm not talking about y'all as kids, but the adults that was able were too mentally distraught that they didn't know how to save her. It's really nobody's fault here, but it's never too late. Have you reached out since you been here?"

"Nawl, can't really find the words to say to her. Plus, nobody has heard from her yet."

"You're a thirty-two-year-old grown ass man now. Step up. Talk to her. The woman just lost a daughter and a nephew. She's had enough space. Do you know where she's at?"

"Nawl, but I know where she lives. Nana said she called, but she still hasn't answered. Aunt Maddy said she went by and rang the doorbell a few times, but she didn't come to the door—"

"And that doesn't worry you? Something could be wrong with her, yet nobody is taking the extra steps to find out. This ain't like the friend I know. He'll go through hell and high waters for the people he loves. Or is this your way of saying that you don't love her now?"

I sat quietly, sipping from my glass. I loved my mom. She was once the queen in my life. I admired everything about her. The way she talked, the way she played with me, the way she taught me how to love— but that changed when she left us. However, as I sat listening to Santana, he'd said things that really touched me and he was right. It was definitely past time that I stepped up.

"Say less bro. Say less."

Santana smiled. "That's the Islande Pierre I know."

"Yo, everybody round here calls me Remy. Nobody uses Islande." I grinned.

"Joe calls you Remy a lot, but it'll grow on me. So, what we doing while I'm here? I know it's hard to wanna enjoy a little, but we gotta do something 'round this bitch."

"We're hitting a lil' spot tonight that my ex owns. It's a club."

"Oooh, so I finally get to meet the infamous Vanessa?"

"I guess so, if she's there." I smiled.

"So, you mentioned you saw her earlier this week but you didn't say how it went."

"Boyyy," I started. We laughed and talked a lil' longer but, as time passed, I knew I had things to do and so did he. I wanted to make sure that I got back in time, so we could get ready for what we'd planned later. I hadn't hit the town in Gainesboro in a long time, and I couldn't lie. I was actually looking forward to it.

As I stood to the door of the house that I was told was my mama's address, my heart pounded damn near out my chest. The house was nice. I could see her living like this. I'd heard she was still doing drugs, but who really knew? The yard didn't look junky, the house looked freshly painted, and a fairly new white Jeep Cherokee was parked in the driveway. I'd say she was doing well for herself. That within itself kind of pissed me off. I would've rather see her drugged the fuck up and out her mind than to see her doing good. Why would she be in this state and not reach out? I mean, damn, she had lost her daughter and her nephew.

"What the fuck?!" I let out, just as the front door opened.

"Islande?" the man said.

I frowned. "Yeah, who are you?"

"I'm Gary."

I looked him over. I didn't know this man from a can of paint. "So, being that you know me, then you must know my mama, Natacha."

He nodded. "Yes, I do."

"Okay, and—"

"Come in."

"Is she here?"

"No, she's not here. I haven't seen her in a few days."

"So, what does that mean?"

"If you come in, I can talk to you about her."

I shook my head. "I'd rather not."

"Well, I'm the guy that your mom has been dealing with for fifteen years."

I just looked at him. I didn't know why I didn't suspect she'd actually have a real life outside of us, but I did. What the hell did he mean he was someone she was dealing with, but she couldn't even deal with her own kids? That shit didn't sit right with me.

"So, where is she?"

"I told you I haven't seen her in days. I don't know. She can't be around here because I know of all the places she would go when she just wants to get away?"

"What you mean, get away?"

"Your mom is a drug addict. She has gotten clean more than a few times, but it doesn't last long. She can't seem to get over losing her sister."

"And my dad," I added with a serious face.

"Him too and, now, she's lost a daughter and a nephew. She'd been clean for more than a year this time around until that happened I believe. She disappeared, and I haven't seen her since. Her phone goes straight to voicemail or she doesn't answer it. She has turned off her tracker, so that leaves me unsure of her whereabouts."

"So, you mean to tell me you've been dealing with a druggie for fifteen years? Why, I mean, what's in it for you? The money?"

He grinned like I'd said something funny, but I was dead ass serious. "I have my own money young man. I take care of your mom, she doesn't take care of me. And truth be told, I love her. I've loved her since the day we met in rehab."

"Oh wow, you're a druggie too."

"Was an addict. But I've been clean for fifteen years. Look around. Do it look like I can't maintain?"

"Nawl, you're definitely maintaining," I told him.

"Your mom always talks about you and your sisters. She has wanted to reach out so many times over the years but doesn't know how y'all would react after—"

"Listen man, I really don't wanna hear this. I got too much on my plate as is. When you see her, just tell her that I came by," I said and turned to walk off. Just as I had made it to my car, I glanced back at him. "Better yet, don't mention I was even here."

As I got in my car and drove away, tears started to fall. I was that close to seeing the woman that gave birth to me, yet, she wasn't there. Dude claimed she'd been clean several times in the years he'd known her, but nan time did she reach out to say anything to me, nothing to any of us. I was her oldest. I could've been there for her. For some reason, I felt like I'd gotten my heart broken all over again. Big mistake, but definitely one I wasn't willing to make twice.

***

I stepped out of my black-on-black Mercedes Maybach feeling fly as fuck. I had a diamond iced-out Audemar Piguet on my wrist, a diamond cut Cuban link chain around my neck, custom ten-thousand-dollar Air Force One sneakers on my feet, designer Celine jeans and a fresh ass matching sweater. The night air was cold, as smoke blew out my mouth just from me breathing.

"Damn, this bitch packed," Santana said, dressed in his Gucci gear.

"Hell yeah," I agreed, looking back at Joe. The nigga was Versace from head to toe. I knew him and Santana didn't come out for no smoke. If anything, they just wanted to find a bad bitch they could take back to the hotel and show 'em what it was like to be fucked by a boss. But I'd had more than a few shots of tequila before getting here. Honestly, I was ready for whatever.

"I think somebody told them we were in town and coming out tonight," he said.

"I agree." I nodded, as we made our way to the door.

"Damn, it's some thick ass women out here. Talk about cornbread fed," Santana cheesed. "Fuck around and I move here for good. Lemme find out my queen in Gainesboro."

We laughed. That nigga was crazy.

"Hey, that's Remy and Joe," two ladies shrieked as they smiled while waving their hands.

We spoke back and, as we stood in the line behind them, I heard one of 'em say, "I told you they was coming home after what happened to their people."

"That shit is so sad."

"You got that right."

"Maybe I can ease one of 'em pain," the other said, looking back at me with a lick of the lips and a seductive smile. "Sorry for your loss."

I nodded my head with a nonchalant expression. "Thanks," I responded. I wasn't here for that. Although, it didn't sound like a bad idea. At this rate, I could definitely use somebody to ease my pain. I grinned at just the thought of entertaining it, but then my smile turned upside down the minute I spotted— muthafuckin' rent a cop standing at the door with a couple other polices as the security. Crab ass nigga just didn't know. I wanted all the smoke. He was lucky I left my Glock in the car. Only because I'd heard that they searched for shit like that before entering. Little did he know, I had dreams of pistol whoopin' his ass.

"You good?" Joe asked, already peeping what I'd seen.

"Yeah, bro." I coolly nodded.

"Joe and Remy. We meet again," he said, as I paid the girl at the counter for us to get in.

"Darnell, right?" I pondered like I ain't know who his pussy ass was.

"Yeah," he replied with a chill smile on his face, as they searched us for weapons. He patted me on the shoulder. "Y'all guys have fun tonight."

I simply nodded my head, entering the club with Joe and Santana following me. I swear, it felt like all eyes were on us. From niggas walking up shaking our hand, to females giggling and pointing, shit, I felt like a fuckin' superstar. I was sure they thought I was because nan nigga I knew in this bitch had money like we did. I was definitely big bank, and the masses knew it. A month ago, never would I have thought I'd be out in my hometown about to get further lit in this bitch.

"Y'all made it." Shakita smiled as she walked up giving me a hug. "Long time no see friend."

"Wassup Kita. It's definitely been a long time," I responded. She hugged Joe, then Santana, even though she didn't know him. "We have a section for y'all."

"Oh, yeah? I didn't know y'all were expecting us?"

"Well, you know bestie said that y'all might come out tonight. So, it was really just in case."

"I see."

"Follow me." She sashayed in front of us, as Santana eyed that fat ass.

"I might hit that tonight," he coolly stated like Kita was already in the bag.

"Shit, go for it." I grinned.

Once we were in the private section that was prepared for us, I noticed a gallon of Hennessy in an ice bucket, a bottle of Remy Martin XO Excellence in another ice bucket, along with a bottle of Gran Patron Platinum. I smiled. The Gran Patron Platinum was what I needed in my life.

We sat down, as the servers came over and poured our drinks. This type of treatment was very common for me. However, getting it here in Gainesboro wasn't exactly how it used to be. For one, there were no clubs with private sections or as nice as this one. We partied in hood spots and drank Jose Cuervo, Crown Royal, Hennessy, Cîroc or other shit. I had a main girl, but I fucked with other bitches. Nessa just stayed down with a nigga, which was the reason why I wanted to marry her. Come to think about it; in a sense, I wasn't no better than Natacha because I'd left her behind too.

"Anybody heard from Wesley?"

"Yeah, he just text and said he and Gaelle are outside," Joe said, glancing down at his phone.

The girls that was in the line ahead of us entered our private section. They wasted no time choppin' it up with Santana and Joe. Guess I seemed uninterested, but it was only one person I really was looking for.

"I'll be back."

"Aye!" Joe called out. "Don't go too far."

"A'ight," I responded.

I headed out the private section into the crowd of people either dancing, mingling or standing against the wall watching everybody. Some were making their way over just wanting a hug or a friendly dap. I felt like a fuckin' celebrity in this bitch, but I ain't have time for the small talk. I was on a mission. As I headed in the bar area, I ran right into Nessa, who was just standing there patrolling the area.

I licked my lips just seeing her fine, thick ass. "Wassup Ma?"

She looked at me with a sweet smile on her face. "Nothing much Islande. I see you made it."

"Kita said the same thing," I teased, pulling her in for a hug.

"Damn, you smell good," she whispered.

"Shit, you the one smelling good." I cheesed. I mean, literally, I couldn't help myself. She just had that effect on me.

"I told bestie that I was hoping y'all would come out."

"I'm glad we did. It's nice as hell in here. Thanks for hooking us up with a private section. I wasn't expecting that."

"You know I got you, regardless—" she paused but never revisited. I guess whatever more she had to say, it wasn't necessary. "I'm happy you're here to see what I've done."

"Nice accomplishment," I congratulated her. "I'm proud of you. This place is everything you talked about when we were growing up."

"I know. I just never imagined it would've been here."

I sipped from my drink, just gazing in her eyes. I could tell a part of her wanted to dwell on the past, but I wasn't gon' let her. "Damn, I just wanna kiss you," I said, clearly throwing her off.

She blushed. "Islande, don't start."

I pushed up on her. "You know I want you."

"Please, it's people in here and they're watching us."

"I don't care. Do you?" I asked, now softly smoochin' around her neck.

"Islaaaande," she lightly sang in my ear, then gently pushed me back and out of her personal space. "You're lit."

"I know." I smiled. "And you ain't. You need to be feeling like me."

"I don't need to get on that level. I might get in trouble tonight."

"I know you don't care about ya lil boyfriend. I'm that nigga, gon' always be that nigga. You know that."

"Hey Remy," some lil' broad said as she walked over.

Instantly, Nessa threw her hand up in the girl's face. "Back up honey, he's taken right now."

I laughed. "How you tryna regulate me when yo' nigga here?"

"Well, get out my face and I won't be regulatin' yo' ass," she teased with a devious smirk.

I sipped a lil' more of my drink. "Come, leave with me."

"Oh, now you want me to leave with you."

"Stop, doing that."

"I'm just sayin' Islande. You ain't been wanting me to leave with you."

"But is it too late?" She dropped her head, not wanting to look in my eyes. I gently grabbed her by the face, making her look at me. "Is it too late?"

"We not doing this. You're drunk."

"I feel good— all that, but not drunk," I assured her. However, I was definitely borderline my limit.

"Come, let me walk you back to your section. You need to be around your people," she said, but I caught on quickly as I scoped my surroundings. I didn't recognize some of the faces there, but I didn't need to. Wesley walked up out of nowhere just in time to catch some nigga approaching me.

"Heard you been asking 'bout me and my brother."

"Nigga, my cousin don't even know yo' ass. Fall the fuck back," Wesley insisted.

"Come on Busy. Don't sweat that shit," the other fella said.

I knew then who they were. But before they could walk off, I noticed a sparkling sapphire diamond bracelet on his wrist that matched the Cuban link chain bedazzled in sapphire diamonds around his neck. It synched perfectly with his blue and white Polo sweater. First thought came to mind was what Miss Martha said about the colors. Before I knew it, I had grabbed him in the neck of his sweater.

"Nigga, was it you?! I'll break yo' muthafuckin' neck in this bitch!"

Everybody started scrambling. Next thing I knew, a nigga had snatched my chain and took off running, but I held that nigga Busy close to me. I wanted his head on a silver platter.

"Nigga, was it you?!"

He swung to get loose but, when he did, I decked that nigga so hard in the face, I damn near knocked him off his feet. From that moment forward, shit seemed a blur. I remember Wesley catching the other one with a swift fist to the face, as they went at it. However, their lil' goons were coming from everywhere with Nico and his lil' goons on their asses. Women were screaming, people were running; Nessa was yelling for me to calm me down, but I was on go.

Somehow, Busy got loose and took off for the club doors. But I was on his ass like back pockets. I already knew where he was going. The second I made it outside, a lil' hitter ran up on me and got knocked the fuck out by Joe. He always had that surprise knockout -energy for an unsuspecting nigga. I rushed behind Busy, catching him as soon as he opened his car door. As I pinned that nigga to his car, I felt a cold piece of iron to the back of my head.

"Turn him loose."

Just that fast, I realized the voice belonged to the pussy cop that was fuckin' my girl. Another police rushed over, as I let Busy go. He grabbed Busy to make sure he wasn't stupid enough to get his piece out.

I turned and looked Darnell straight in the eyes. "You only get one chance to pull a gun on me."

"Is that a threat?"

"It's a promise," I responded.

"Turn around," he told me. I did as he said. I figured this was the part when he'd put his handcuffs on me but, to my surprise, he didn't take it that far.

"Aye, pussy nigga! Get yo' muthafuckin' hands off my cousin!" Wesley snapped but, just that fast, a police officer was on his ass too. I looked over to see Joe and Santana had made it to my car. Joe was definitely about to air this bitch out— until...

"Talk to yo' peeps," Rent a cop said, having already peeped the scene.

I just stared over at 'em with a shake of the head. Joe caught the look.

"Darnell, give him a break. He just lost his sister and cousin," Nessa pleaded.

Darnell wasn't tryna hear that shit. I was sure a part of him wanted my ass on the first flight outta here anyway. Especially, how I was not long ago feeling up on his supposed to be girl in front of everybody. He put my ass in the backseat of the police car and got in the front.

"So, you really gon' do this?" I asked.

"You gon' learn tonight," he griped while starting the engine on his car.

I glanced down at my wrist. "Muthafucka!" I let out. My damn watch was gone.

"That's what happens when you show up to a hood party looking like a billion dollars."

Hood party? I pondered to myself. "Ain't you on the door? Keep the muthafuckin' hood out the party."

"Knew I shouldn't have let you in," he mocked.

I smugly grinned with a shake of the head. I'd let him have that. "What they tryna do to my cousin?" I asked, as I saw Wesley and two police officers exchanging words.

"They gon' either let him go or you'll see him in the holding cell next to you."

"Nigga, you lame as fuck," I uttered.

"What you said?" he asked, mean mugging me in the rear-view mirror.

I simply shook my head but, as we were pulling out the parking lot, somebody started lettin' off 'rounds. Shit sounded like explosives going off.

"Get down!" Darnell yelled.

Glass flew in on me, as I ducked for cover. I saw blood on my hand, as an awkward pain suddenly hit me. "What the fuck?!" I yelled, as loud screams on the outside pierced my ears.

Darnell jumped out the car to check the scene. "Oh shit. I need help! He's hit!"

VANESSA "NESSA" LUCAS

While at my house pacing back and forth with all types of thoughts going through my mind, my phone rang. Expecting a couple of calls from anybody at this point since I didn't know what was really going on, I quickly answered.

"Hello."

"Hey Nessa, this Maddy. I know it's early as hell, but Joe called mama and said that Wesley and Remy were taken to jail. Um—he mentioned that he and Santana were heading there as well. However, Joe's phone is now going to voicemail and Gaelle ain't answering hers either. Do you know what's going on?"

"I don't know. Instead of going to the jail, I came on home."

"So, do you know anything?"

I shrugged as if she could see me. "It's a bunch of chaos surrounding their arrests. Remy got into it with two brothers that he felt had something to do with Lovely and James' murder. Of course, Wesley was close by and jumped in. That fight started several fights inside my club and, then, it led outside to where more fights broke out. Luckily, I have police on duty, and they did what they were hired to do. However, I feel like Darnell was targeting Islande because of our past history."

"That figures," Maddy sighed.

"Don't get me wrong. Islande wasn't exactly innocent, but he didn't have to be hauled off to jail either."

"I understand. So, Josette got a call that somebody got shot. Who was it?"

"Some dude that had ran up to Darnell's police car-"

"Why would he do that?"

"Apparently, the dude was trying to shoot Islande. At least that's what the talk was about after some of the commotion had ceased."

"Why would he want to shoot Remy?"

"I don't know Maddy. This shit is crazy. Nevertheless, the police peeped it and shot him first. Remy wasn't hurt, besides the glass that blew in on him during the shots fired. However, I won't know too much more until I talk to Darnell. He's not answering his phone either, but I'm sure it's just a matter of time before he calls or comes over. Hopefully, by then, Islande and Wesley will be released."

"Yeah, hopefully, because Mama is worried. Plus, you know we lay Lovely and James to rest in the morning at ten."

"I know. That's why I was trying to tell Darnell to chill out and be a lil' mo' understanding."

"Yeah, he took it too far."

"I'll deal with him soon enough."

"Anyway, how are things with you and Remy?"

"After that big blow-out at y'all's house, we didn't speak no more. Honestly, I didn't even see him until he showed up at the club. But I was hoping that he'd come out. You know, to see my club and all. I just hate it turned out the way it did. I'm just thankful that the police intervened before something bad happened to Islande."

"Yeah, we wouldn't have been able to handle that." Maddy said. "So, how is the boy that got shot?"

"He left in the back of an ambulance. I have no clue what's going on with that. Nor do I know who the hell he is."

"Do you think he could've had something to do with—"

I shrugged again, already knowing where she was going with this. "Don't get me to lyin' because I honestly don't know. We'll get answers soon enough, I'm sure," I said as I heard my front door opening. "I'll call you back Maddy."

"Don't forget and especially if you hear something."

"I won't," I said and quickly ended the call. I didn't want her saying or asking nothing else. I needed to know what was going on, probably even more so than she did.

"Who were you on the phone with?"

"Why is that your concern?" I asked, feeling even more pissed off that this nigga would have the nerves to walk in here questioning me like he ain't already crossed several boundaries.

"I see you're still mad," he said, pulling his jacket off and throwing it across the back of the sofa.

"And is."

He heavily sighed. "Babe, you know he deserved to go jail for his behavior and let's not mention his total disrespect and regards for me being there—"

"Meaning?"

"All over you in the club like he didn't know you belonged to me."

"I belong to nobody," I said, holding up my ring finger. "Yes, we date, but we're not engaged or married."

"See, you're tryna be technical here and I'm just saying that everybody that knows us knows that we're a couple. Are you going to argue about that too?"

"I'm not arguing about nothing— yet."

"Well, beat yo' chest then. I'm listening."

"Islande only got into that brawl because he believes that those guys have something to do with his people's murders. Mind you, murders that y'all can't seem to solve."

"Don't come for me or my job Nessa."

"Why not? You're coming for me and the people I love—" My eyes widened just as those words escaped my lips.

"The people you love, or it is the man you love?"

"Does that matter?"

"Hell yeah, it matters! That nigga been gone for ten years and pops back up only because of death in his family, yet you're allowing him to be all over you like he never left or hurt you. Make it make sense Nessa!"

"It doesn't have to make sense to you, but it does to me. Yes, it's been ten years. Do I forgive him for leaving me like that? No! But you're not gonna sit in my face and tell me how to feel about a situation or a man when you know nothing of my true feelings," I spat with an irritated heart.

"What are your true feelings? Are you still in love?"

"No."

"So, why let him disrespect you in the club like that?"

"He didn't disrespect me."

"So, you don't think I felt disrespected to have people coming to me about the shit?"

"I get it, I do, and maybe I was caught up in the moment. I apologize about that, but you were being a straight asshole for arresting him."

"He was fighting. What more did you want me to do? What he really wanted was gunplay. You knew it."

"Yet, you still didn't have to arrest him. His sister and cousin will be laid to rest in the morning. That's why I said to just let it go, let him go. If you weren't so cold and in your feelings about him being in my face inside the club, you would've listened. Arresting him wasn't the answer."

"I didn't arrest him. Neither of them were arrested."

"Huh?"

"Yeah, huh?" he mocked.

I stood, not really knowing what to say next. I'd already planned out a whole thought processed argument in my head, but that seemed to have changed the minute he said he didn't arrest Islande. "You didn't?"

"No, I didn't. Him and Wesley were actually taken down to the station for their protection. Clearly, there was more going on than they really knew. The fight that broke out between him and the brothers was nothing compared to what was waiting on the outside. I get he felt they had something to do with the murders of his people, but they didn't. We've been watching them for a while. They are actually under federal investigation. They had nothing to do with that."

"How you know?"

"I said we've been watching them, Nessa. They had no motive or real reason to have James and Lovely murdered. Islande can't just show up and think he has it all figured out because he has money. We'll find out who did this to his people. I promise we will."

As bad as I hated even asking now, I had no choice. "Well, that was Maddy on the phone and she said that Mrs. Pierre is worried. Is there any news I can give them?"

"I left them at the jail but I'm sure by now they should be at their destinations. Or at least getting ready to leave the station anyway. Islande had questions for the investigators. I didn't feel I needed to stick around for that. Plus, I knew I had to get here, so we could talk."

"Well, thanks for thinking of me because I was definitely in my feelings."

"I know."

"But, you're right. You were only doing your job at the club. Had it been anybody else, I wouldn't have said nothing. That is true. I only stepped in though because of the situation that's surrounding them."

"I know," Darnell said. "I don't wanna think we'll have problems while Islande is here. Will we?"

"What do you mean?" I frowned.

"I know you'll want to spend time with him before he leaves. I trust you to do that but amicably, nothing more or less. But if you feel that you may want to travel back in time and explore your options, then please tell me."

"Darnell, why are you talkin' like this?"

"Because I'm no fool and I don't wanna be treated as one either."

"I understand, but there is nothing that Islande and I have to explore. That is in the past and it'll stay there," I said, as Darnell just looked over at me. I could see in his eyes that he didn't believe me.

"Guess I'll have to take your word for it."

"Please do. But—" I said with hesitance.

"No buts, just don't play me for a fool," he reminded me.

"I'm not," I said, as he grabbed his jacket and put it back on. "Where are you going?"

"I'm going home now."

"Oh, you're not staying here?"

"Nah, I need to clear my head. I had a long night," he answered.

"You still could've stayed here though."

"I think it's best that I leave. I'll call when I wake up. You can call Mrs. Pierre and let her know what's going on, just in case the guys are still at the station. I'll talk to you later."

"Oh wow," I mumbled. Darnell didn't give me so much as a peck on the cheek. That definitely wasn't how he'd usually leave me. I was sure he was a bit pissed at how things went down. I didn't make it no better letting Remy kiss all over my damn neck like that. I didn't know what the hell I was thinking. Maybe it was the few shots of Patron I'd had before arriving. Or it could've been old feelings surfacing. Who knew? A part of me wanted to blame it on the liquor but, truth be told, I still had feelings. *Damn.* I hated to be so vulnerable for a nigga that really left me like a bad habit but, for some reason, he still had a hold on me. A hold that I had to watch because the last thing I needed was to fall all over again, already knowing that his ass wasn't gon' catch me.

I walked over to the door as I watched Darnell get in his patrol car and wasted no time leaving out of my driveway. I felt bad because I knew a part of him was hurt that I disregarded his feelings. Clearly, I did, and I knew better. I knew what it felt like to be hurt. Hell, the nigga that hurt me was the same nigga I was allowing in to hurt him. *Damn.*

Instead of dwelling on what had happened, I called Mrs. Pierre instead. On the first ring, she answered.

"Hello."

"Mrs. Pierre, have you heard anything yet?"

"No, not yet. Have you?"

"Yes ma'am," I answered. "Darnell just left here and said that Islande and Wesley weren't arrested. However, when he left the station, Islande was speaking with the detectives about the progress of their investigation on what happened."

"Well, thank God. I knew they wouldn't have had to sit long but it's the principle of it all. I don't want them getting hemmed up in any trouble. Remy has come a long way from his past. I'd hate for him to return, home only to be caught back up in the same shit he left for."

"I agree," I said, fixing myself a mimosa. Shit, I needed something stronger than this, but it was only four o' clock in the morning and considered to be early as shit for some. However, on a good night, I'd just be making it home from closing down the club and preparing for bed to be snuggled up with my man.

"You alright baby?"

"Yes ma'am," I responded with reservation.

"You don't sound like it."

I heavily sighed. "I just have things on my mind."

"Remy?"

"Yeah, mostly."

"Listen, don't let Remy coming home get your hopes up too high. I know it's been ten years and maybe this time has opened his eyes to wanting more. But who knows where his head is really at? Remy has changed a lot. Plus, you have a new life with a—"

"Yeah, I know," I cut her off, not wanting her to get on that subject because it always led to more anytime she mentioned it.

"You know I love you like one of my own and the last thing I want is for you to get hurt again—"

"I know."

"So, you can't allow him to come back in unless he's sure and I mean certain that you're what he really wants. Meaning, this time, he won't leave you behind. Ironically, I always say that he's a lot like his mom. He runs and hides from what he thinks are his problems. When, in actuality, his problems are his savior. He just doesn't or shall I say can't see it. Yes, it's unfortunate but, like Natacha, he has to learn the hard way. I miss my daughter. I don't know how she's handling the loss of her daughter and her nephew. It broke her to lose her twin sister. You would've really had to know how close they were to each other to understand that void in her life. They shared the same womb, finished each other's sentences, did each other's hair, talked for hours on the phone when they couldn't be around each other— they were like two peas in a pod so, when Joseph took Nadia's life, that broke her. Not only was her sister gone, but she also lost the love of her life. Ramirez would give Natacha the world. He loved her wholeheartedly, her and the kids. This is why she wasn't present when it happened. Ramirez wouldn't let her go with him to pick them up. Thank God, he didn't because Joseph had plans that nobody knew about except him."

I could hear her tone shaky as she paused to gather herself but then continued.

"He took my baby. He took my son-n-law. He stripped my daughter of a happy life and, honestly, our family hasn't been the same since. Yes, we've made it look easy over the years, but it's been the hardest thing ever to keep it together. Life has forced us to deal with the unexpected in the harshest way ever and, now, we're back with these same feelings that suddenly resurfaced on that exact same day as twenty-three years ago."

Tears filled my eyes. I could hear the pain in her voice. I knew how she felt. I saw how that effected Islande and everybody else in their family. I was there with them. I experienced what they were dealing with, and it was nothing nice. I had the upmost respect for their family because I didn't know if mine could've handled it the way they did. Somehow, they managed to get through it, and Mrs. Pierre was the glue that held them together. She was indeed a superwoman, and I admired her for that.

"Wow," she continued." "I'm still in disbelief, yet I'm trying to be strong for my family. But, this shit hurts like hell. I'm so discouraged right now but I have to be strong for my family. They can't lose me too."

"I know, Mrs. Pierre. But try to stay strong."

"Whoever did this knows deep down how to hit us. This was so personal on so many levels and it's sickening. Whomever is behind this is a sick muthafucka. They are the weakest link on this earth to stoop as low as this. This is beyond anything that I could've ever imagined."

"I know."

"And whatever happens to them is going to be between them and God. Only He can fix this and, in my soul, I know He will, one day."

"You're right."

"Tomorrow morning is gon' be hard for all of us. Are you coming? You're one of us, don't forget that."

"Uh—" I hesitated.

"Regardless of what you and Remy got going on, you have to come. We've kept in touch since he's been gone. You've been my rock even during the year and a half you disappeared."

For some reason, I just knew she was going to mention that.

"I just need to see your loving face. I need you to be there. Please—"

"I'll be there. I'll come," I assured her, just as my doorbell rang. "Mrs. Pierre, somebody is at my door," I said.

"Who is it?" she nosily pondered.

"I don't know. I haven't went yet."

"Well, go," she said like she ran my house.

Damn. "Okay den," I uttered, making my way to the door. I peeped through the peephole and gasped a little.

"Is that my child?" she questioned, like she could see through my damn peephole.

"Yes ma'am," I told her.

"Okay," she said. "Let him in, but don't forget what I told you. And tell his ass to call me the second he leaves," she said followed by "Oh, this Joe calling. I'll talk to you later baby. Love you."

"Love you too, Mrs. Pierre."

I opened the door with an anxious heart.

"You don't wanna let me in?" he asked, standing before me looking like a billion dollars.

"Islande, I could've had company."

"But you don't," he casually responded, looking around as if he was looking for another car besides mine.

"Lemme guess— Mrs. Pierre told you where I lived?"

"Yeah, is that a problem?"

"No."

"Why you living way out here anyway? Your club is in the city, but you're damn near in the next town over."

"I have my reasons. What you want?" I asked, trying to stand my ground, even though his presence always had a way of breaking me down.

"Can I come in?"

I hesitated as I stood in the doorway and watched him, not knowing what to respond. I glanced back over my shoulder. It was things I didn't need him questioning if he stepped inside my house.

"Well— um—"

"Okay, well, come sit in the car with me then. I need someone I can trust to talk to."

"Really Islande?"

"Yes, come on," he coolly said, gently grabbing me by the hand as I followed him to his car. I didn't know what this unexpected, unusually early as hell visit was about, but a part of me had to get my shit together spiritually and mentally because no damn telling. As we made it to his car, he turned and looked at me with the saddest eyes ever. Damn near made me tear up just watching him.

"What's wrong Islande?"

He shook his head like he couldn't find the words to say.

"Babe, what's wrong?"

"She was pregnant. She was pregnant and they did my sister like that."

I was speechless. The only thing I could do was gently wrap my arms around his neck, so he could cry on my shoulder. I felt so bad for him, for the family and for the situation. I didn't know if they'd ever get over this or even heal from it all. But, whoever did this shit was some fucked up individuals and, if Remy had something to do with it, they were going to pay for this one way or the fuckin' other.

ISLANDE "REMY" PIERRE

I laid across the bed thinking that the night couldn't have gone any worse than it had. How the fuck I end up in a situation that led to my ass going to jail? Mind you, by the nigga that was fuckin' the woman I once was deeply in love with. Luckily, he wasn't arresting me but more like probably saving my life.

Thoughts began to really flood my mind. Who the fuck was that lil' young nigga that pulled a gun out on me? I swear, everything I'd ever did good and bad flashed before me. I found myself staring down the barrel of a gun through the window of a cop car. Thank God, another cop was on alert and shot his ass before he shot me. Now, I had to figure out who the hell he was and why he felt like killing me was in his best interest.

One thing I knew for certain was that he was definitely involved in some kind of way with the murders surrounding Lovely and James. I had a gut feeling about this shit and it was strong as hell. All we needed was to talk to him as soon as possible. However, the detectives were adamant about handling this on their own and, as soon as the guy was able, they'd question him to find out his motive. Nah, they had better be sitting by his bed because I was gon' stalk that bitch out, so I could get to his ass first.

"Yo, you good in here?" Santana asked as he peeked his head in my room door.

"Nah man. I'm still furious. I just want answers, and the only thing I've found out so far is that Lovely was six months pregnant and a pussy nigga shot her eleven times. Not to mention, my cousin could've lived but a nigga got out the vehicle, stood over him and shot him in the fuckin' head. That video we saw was grainy, but I could see the shit clear as day."

"Yeah, that was really fucked up."

"She was pregnant man. Damn. She was pregnant," I said as a tear fell from my eyes.

"I know man. Just reading over the autopsy report had me stunned."

"I know Royal had already said it, but I don't even wanna tell Nana that it was confirmed. Shit heartbreaking. They couldn't have known or at least they didn't care. I mean, were they after James and she was just a casualty of war? None of this shit is adding up or making sense to me."

"From the way the nigga stepped out the vehicle and shot James, I'd say it was targeted but for him. I think Lovely and Wesley were casualties. Fortunately, Wesley survived. I mean, think about it. He was in the backseat, but most of the shots were fired in the front. The only way James got caught like that was because he'd been shot a few times before that fatal shot—"

"It's crazy how they said the bullets that hit him weren't life threatening, but the one to the dome is what took him out."

"Yeah, that's fucked up."

"But, you're right. Somebody wanted him dead. I really thought it was dem niggas we were fighting at the club, but the investigators are adamant that they aren't. It only leaves the Cannons but, if Lovely was pregnant by Rod and they were supposedly in love, I don't see him doing her like that."

"Trust me, I've seen a lot of weird shit in my time of being a private investigator. It could've been him." Santana shrugged.

I nodded. "You're right. It could've been him, but that's the thing that has me so stumped. That beef been over a long time ago. He was never really a part of it. He was just the brother of the niggas we had beef with. I mean, was this all a plan to get back at me for killing his brother?"

"It could be."

"Did he stoop that low to have her fall in love with him just so he could get her pregnant and then kill her?"

"I don't know, but I've seen muthafuckas do worse for get back."

"Wow, I got a fuckin' headache just thinking about this shit."

"I know. Hell, me too," he said, firing up a blunt. He passed it to me. "Here, take the edge off a little."

I hit the blunt a couple of times, thoughts all over the place.

"How did it go when you went to see Vanessa?"

I shrugged, hitting the blunt again.

"After ten years nigga, you still love that woman."

"I do, but I was no good for her back then. I knew it. I didn't wanna drag her miles away from home only to disappoint her. Yeah, I played it raw by just cuttin' her off cold turkey and leaving her at the altar. I was wrong as fuck for that shit. You know I think about it often."

"I know."

"But, by the time I realized that I had fucked up, it was too late to reach out. I figured she'd never forgive me, so I just let it be. It wasn't no need to beg her back only for me to still be running the streets, cause I wasn't ready."

"I feel you."

"I still love her, though."

"So, if she was into you like that, would you be with her?"

"I would. I'm at a point where I feel like settling down could only enhance my life. You know I get tired of the back and forth with women. Yeah, it's all fun, don't get me wrong, but only for the moment. That's the catch 22 because when it's over, it's over until the next time. However, it would be nice to wake up to the same woman every morning—"

Santana bust out laughing.

I simply shook my head. "Yeah, I might be lyin'," I joked.

"I know."

"But seriously— I don't know. So much time has passed, it's hard to say. Plus, I don't know if she's in that headspace. She was definitely here for me earlier in ways I don't think nobody else could've been. She knows me. That won't change just because we've been out of each other's lives for ten years."

"Shit, I get it. You've always spoken highly of her, and you definitely keep up with her social media accounts."

"Got to, but she ain't never posted a nigga on her page. She don't even change her relationship status. Hell, I know she fuckin' but it couldn't have been that serious. Even now with rent-a-cop ol' hatin' ass, she can't love that nigga. I know it. I could tell if she was, but she ain't."

"You should know."

"Damn right I should, and I do," I responded, just as a knock was heard at the door. I looked over at Santana. "That's probably Joe or Wesley."

"Wesley's lady was taking him home, so I highly doubt it's him but definitely Joe or Marla."

I got up and headed to the door, didn't even peek out the peephole; I just opened it. My eyes lit up but only because I was surprised as hell by this unexpected company.

"Baby, how you feeling? Why didn't you call me?"

"Um—" Instantly, Regan wrapped her arms around me.

"I'm so sorry to hear about your sister and your cousin. You should've called me."

I frowned with unsure emotions. "How did you find out?"

"Iesha told me when I called her last night. She thought I knew."

"Oh."

"I should've known Islande. You could've called me. This situation is big; I should be here by your side through a time like this."

"Well— you know we aren't exactly together. It's been what— um— three months or so?"

"More like two but who's counting?"

"Me," I answered with a shake of the head. I didn't even expect her to pop up like this, let alone show up to my room without letting me know but, as always, that's how Regan rolled. She moved how she wanted to, which was why she and I would go our separate ways at any given time.

"Anywaysss," she sang, clearly ignoring me. "Are you ok?" she asked, caressing my face.

"Nawl, but I will be."

"Damn, this is so sad. I wanted to call you, but I figured I'd just jump on my father's private jet and get here as fast as I could."

"Oh."

"Aren't you happy to see me?"

"I guess."

"Does anything look different about me?" she asked, twirling in a circle.

"You got your nose done?" I pondered, now staring at her face.

"No, must be my make-up. You know I have a new make-up artist now."

"Nawl, I didn't know but you get a new one every other month."

"Well— I like to change it up a little every now and then."

"Oh, I know."

"Guess again," she said, now turning so I could see that juicy wagon she was draggin'.

"That ass lookin' fatter."

She grinned. "Yezzz, my fat ass is perfect now. Feel it. It's so soft and jiggly. It looks so natural, don't it?"

I grinned a little, but it wasn't because I loved her fat ass— I mean, I loved it but that was beside the point. It was just because she spent money on bullshit and the unnecessary. She was already fine when I met her some five-six years ago, but one surgery led to another and then she'd find something else to get nipped and tucked. It was just getting ridiculous. She was only twenty-seven years old. Definitely beautiful but was bird-brained like a muthafucka. I always blamed her parents for that. She was just a spoiled lil' princess that ran them and anybody else she could get over.

"You like it?"

I nodded my head. "Yeah, it's nice."

"Ohh, I'm sorry. Here I am rambling about my ass when, clearly, this is not the time."

"You got that right," Santana acknowledged as he exited the bedroom.

Regan tooted up her nose. "I should've known he was here."

Santana grinned. "And to think, I was two seconds away from asking about you."

I softly chuckled. Santana and Regan weren't the best of friends. They really didn't care for each other. Regan felt like I showed Santana more love than I showed her, and Santana just didn't like her spoiled, self-centered ways. Nevertheless, whenever they were in the same space, they really didn't hold back their feelings for one another.

"Can you believe I had to find out about this from Iesha?"

"Yeah," Santana responded as he joined us in the sitting area of the suite and sat down. "My nigga ain't talked to you in months."

"Whatever Santana." She fanned him off. "That's because he didn't want to. And well— I don't kiss ass. I like mine kissed but, after calling and texting a few times with no answer, I just spend money and forget about it. He'll come around."

"Oh really?" I pondered, shooting her ass an irritated stare.

"Seriously, this is not cool Islande. We've been through too much for you to not reach out about this."

"Again, we aren't together. This is not your problem and has absolutely nothing to do with you."

"But I'm still going to be here for you when you need me."

"Who said he needed you?"

"Santana, don't start with me. Now ain't the time for that either," she sassed with a slick roll of the eyes.

"You right," he said, standing up and stretching his arms out. "Let me know when you ready to get out. I'm gonna head to my room and find out some information. Afterwards, I need to get a lil' rest."

"A'ight," I told him as we dapped each other up.

"You need to try and get some rest too. Tomorrow morning will be here before you know it."

"You right but I can't sleep, especially now." I sighed while looking at Regan. "But call me when you wake up."

"Definitely," he said and walked out. He didn't even acknowledge Regan no more.

"I'm glad he's gone. Always fuckin' up the vibes."

"Regan, don't do that," I said, walking back in the bedroom and falling across the bed. She followed me, sitting in the lounge chair next to the bed.

"Do you want me to stay with you cause I haven't gotten a room yet?"

"Nawl, I need all the space I can get right about now."

"Wow, I fly all this way to be with you and we can't even share a room?"

"I didn't ask you to come here though. I have enough on my mind. I don't need your presence to add to it."

"Wow, it's like that Islande?"

"I'm just sayin' Regan. You know how you are."

"It's been months since we've seen or spoken to each other. The vibes should be good between us now."

"So, you think? But that's not exactly how it is. I'm not thinking about no vibes. I'm thinking 'bout my family and how we're going to get through tomorrow. Hell, even today," I added. "I'm thinking 'bout the killers and what they must be doing right now. I'm thinkin' 'bout moving back here to be closer to Nana. I ain't thinkin' 'bout yo' ass or them weird ass vibes you bring to the table."

"Hold up, you're thinking about moving back to this lil' country ass town?"

I just looked at her. It was times like this that made me wonder how the hell I managed to date her ass for so long. It had to be her looks, her body and that wet, tight pussy because I promise it was nothing else. Shawty had me fucked up a lot of times, I just let her ass slide.

"I don't mean it like that babe. I'm just saying, this ain't your speed no more. You're an up-north type of guy now. You left the filthy south for a reason."

"Filthy?" I frowned.

"I meant dirty or whatever y'all be calling it."

I simply shook my head. "This is my hometown. This is where I'm from. I've never acted like I was better than coming home. I just didn't for personal reasons."

"Yeah, and those personal reasons should have your ass on the next jet smoking when all of this is over."

"Do you think it's over? Do you think this will ever be over? You don't have a clue what it's like to lose someone close to you. You haven't experienced that part of life yet, so you can't sit in here and tell me what I need to be doing when something is over."

"Okaaay babe. Calm down. I'm sorry. You're right. Sometimes, I do speak on things I know nothing about. I shouldn't be sayin' nothing, just consoling you." She plopped down on the bed beside me. "Seriously, I'm jet legged. I just wanna get a lil' rest myself. Please, just let me lay here for a while. I promise to get my own room when I get up."

I frowned, now thinking a lil' clearly about her ass being here. "How the hell you even knew what room I was in?"

"I just tipped the front desk an extra four-hundred dollars to accommodate me."

"I gotta see who this is. I'm gon' report they ass."

She grinned. "Don't do that girl like that. She looked like she needed the extra cash anyway."

I simply shook my head, but I was definitely gon' check their asses 'bout that. "Where yo' bags at? I know you didn't travel this far without any."

"They're in the trunk of the rental car I had reserved when I landed."

"Oh okay. You can get some rest because now that I'm laying here, I'm feeling it coming down on me too. We'll talk more when we get up."

"Okay." She smiled, trying to lie on my back.

"Aye man, move yo' ass over."

"Okaaay," she playfully sang. "You ain't gotta be so rude."

I closed my eyes. If I was going to cruise the city in search for answers, I definitely needed a lil' rest. The last thing I wanted was to be distracted by Regan's ass being here. "Come to think about it, how long you staying?"

"However long you're stayin'."

"Lies you fuckin' tell."

She laughed like it was funny. "Islandeee."

"Islande my ass," I grunted. Without saying another word, I rolled over and dozed off to sleep.

———◦◦◦◦◦———

We pulled up to Fran's Breakfast Bar, as I checked out the area. It was definitely nice as hell. Royal had made a really sweet investment. The outside was inviting with a laid-back seating area, one side with umbrella tables and the other side with a closed-in area. I could see the eighty-inch TV on the wall that Royal bragged to me about from the car.

"This joint is really set up like a sports bar," Santana said.

"Yeah, Royal and Fran put a lot of work in this place," Wesley added.

"And a lot of money." I nodded. "I can tell by the details of the work done to the construction of the building and the landscaping around it. The sign is very inviting and blinged the fucked out. That blue and gray is poppin' in the letters. The bling sets it off."

Wesley laughed. "You know Royal loves herself some indigo blue and bling."

"I think we all love blue, only because that was dad's favorite color," I chimed in with sorted memories of how he'd make sure that he and I dressed alike, especially on weekends or outings being that I was the only son. We would be fresh as hell in our blue Polo shirts or Tommy Hilfiger outfits.

"Lil' cousin definitely had a plan. She'd say ever since she was little that she wanted to own a restaurant and her dreams have come true." Joe smiled.

"Why she named it Fran's Breakfast Bar though?" Santana pondered.

"Fran is one of her best friends. They've been close since jits. Fran had the skills in the kitchen and Royal had the funds and the vision. Together, they put in the work and this is what became of that dream."

"Your lil' sister got a head on her shoulders. That's wassup." Santana smiled, opening the car door. "Come on. Shit, I'm hungry. Been in that room sleep all fuckin' day."

I grinned. "I know right. I didn't even know they opened on Sundays."

"They're open every day of the week. They just open after three on Sundays, serving dinner instead of breakfast," Wesley confirmed.

"That's smart," I said, following the guys in the restaurant. We were seated outside in the enclosed area, so we could see the football game playing. It was just a little past seven and I hadn't ate shit all day. The sleep I'd gotten was much needed.

"Yo, so Regan is here?" Joe asked.

"Yeah, Iesha told her what happened, and she felt the need to show her support, so she say."

"You know I spoke to Iesha about that when she made it here."

"When she got here?" Wesley asked.

"A couple of hours ago. She thought I was 'bout to sit in that room with her ass. Hell nawl. I told her she can go to Nana's if she wanted to get out. The driver will take her anywhere she wants to go."

"So, what did she decide to do?"

"She and Marla are going to Nana's. I told her we'll come later," Joe responded.

"Gaelle is over there too, so that's good. I'm sure she could use the distraction. Her and Josette just don't fuckin' get along."

I laughed. "Yeah, they had some weird shit going on once upon a time."

"You telling me," Wesley laughed. "Hopefully, auntie can keep 'em apart until I get back there."

"Nana has been pressing me about staying there, but I need my space. I haven't been in a house that full of people since our last vacation. Hell, come to think about it, those are the only times I'm in a house full of people."

"Well, at least we're all kin."

"You're right," I commented, as Fran walked over with a big smile on her face.

"Wow, it's been a long time since I've seen you two in the flesh. Give me a hug," she said, as me and Joe stood up to hug her.

"Wow, Francine Barnes, you're not a little girl anymore."

"Nope." She grinned. "I'm a grown ass woman now."

"That you are," Santana chimed in with a smile on his face.

"Hey handsome. What's yo' name?"

"I'm Santana. I hear this is your place. It's nice as hell in here."

"Thank you," she blushed then directed her attention at Wesley. "Wassup crazy?"

Wesley laughed. "Wassup Fran. What you back there whipping up today?"

"Yeah, we want the special." Santana cheesed.

"Oh, I got something special for you, alright." Fran winked.

"Damn, you are grown," Joe laughed.

"I told you. I'm all woman now," she chuckled. "Anywayssss, today's special is oxtails over white rice or mash potatoes, whichever you prefer. Collard greens, potato souffle, mac and cheese and our famous hoe cake."

"Hoe cake?" Santana frowned.

We laughed.

"That's skillet fried cornbread. Looks like a pancake."

Santana grinned. "I knew that."

"Yeah, right. You don't know nothing about this dirty south cookin'," Wesley joked.

"I'm bout to find out though," he chuckled. "Lemme get all that."

"Rice or mash potatoes?"

"I want the rice."

"What do you want to drink? We have really good, sweet tea, Kool-Aid— today, we have the grape and orange kind. It comes with fresh fruit in it—"

"That shit be so fuckin' good," Wesley chimed in.

"Tell 'em." Fran nodded with arrogance.

"Marla been coming here since we arrived," I laughed. "She can't get enough of the Kool-Aid."

"Yeah, she asked if I'd make her a personal pitcher yesterday."

We laughed.

"Damn, well, let me get the orange Kool-Aid."

"Got you," she said, punching in his order on her iPad.

"Did you make Marla the pitcher of Kool-Aid?" I pondered.

"I surely did. We don't turn down money around here."

"You got that right," Royal chimed in as she walked up. "Wassup lil' uglies."

We laughed while speaking to my lil' sis.

"It's nice as hell in here. The way you described the place didn't do it any justice."

"Thanks, bruh. That means a lot coming from you."

"Let me get the rest of y'all orders," Fran butted in.

"Uh—" Royal tugged on my shirt. "Lemme holla at you right quick."

I glanced up at her. "Okay," I said, getting up from my seat.

"You don't need me for anything do you, Royal?" Fran asked.

"Nawl, you can finish taking their orders. I'll be in the kitchen to help you out since we're short staffed today."

"Okay cool," Fran said as she went back to taking orders. Royal and I stepped outside. I didn't know what she wanted to discuss with me. But, from the look on her face, it had to be important, and I couldn't wait to find out what it was about.

ROYAL "SWEETS" PIERRE

"I'm glad we stepped outside to talk, Sweets. I know I wished you a happy birthday and had your convertible Audi R8 delivered that you've been hinting 'round for—"

"Whew! To see them pull that off the truck had me floored. I already knew it came from you before you even called me. I love my fuckin' car. I know I've said thank you every day since I got it but thank you!."

He grinned. "You know I got you. I just wanted to make the day special, not even knowing that we'd be reliving the same grief from twenty-three years ago."

"I know right," I sad with a saddened tone.

"Yo—" he said, looking around the joint. "Sweets, you really outdid yourself with this layout. I love it here."

I smiled. It felt good hearing shit like this from my big brother. "You don't know how that makes me feel. It's like all I've ever wanted was your approval."

"Well, you got it. I'm truly proud of the businesswoman you've become."

"Thank you."

"So, you help out round here too?"

"Yeah, especially when we're short-staffed. That's usually on the weekends. However, I'm starting to think that maybe we can use a couple of days off and so those days will likely be on a Monday and a Tuesday, starting next month. We'll probably open for breakfast only on those days. I'm still thinking it through. Anyways, we've made a killing at this place. Big Chick and Lil' Chick don't stand a chance."

"I bet they don't." He grinned.

"But, hey, we do leave the fried chicken up to them. That's their specialty and we don't wanna run 'em completely outta business," I arrogantly teased. "You know we respect our elders 'round here."

He smiled. "As you should. So, the menu here is breakfast and soul food?"

"Yeah, we don't do fried chicken, burgers or French fries, not even for the kids. They can have chicken fingers with sweet potato fries."

"That's smart."

"But we do have soul food kiddie meals or breakfast kiddie meals. Of course, breakfast is our specialty being that we open at six and don't shut breakfast down til around 1 'ish. Then, we start cooking dinner at two."

"Damn, that's wassup. It's certainly different."

"I know. Nobody 'round here is doing it like us. Yeah, you have places like McDonald's and Burger King serving breakfast but not as long as us and definitely not as good. We do real breakfast, sandwiches and all. Yeah, Huddle House is on the other side of town but they ain't gettin' business like us either."

"I can tell. Everything about this place stands out. I'm glad you put your money to good use."

"Me too." I nodded with a smile.

"So, wassup? What's on yo' mind?"

"First thing— we changed the time of the service in the morning?"

"Huh?" He frowned.

"It'll be at eight instead of ten."

"Eight in the morning? Who does that?"

"We does that," she mocked. "With everything going on, we had to move the time up. I didn't want to push the date back because the sooner we get this over with, the sooner we can all start the process of healing."

"Healing may never come."

"Tis' true, I can't argue with you about that. I'll never get over losing Lovely. She was truly my best friend. She wholeheartedly supported me and my dreams and did not play about her lil' sister. You hear me?"

He grinned. "Yeah, I know. She was always the protective one."

"Definitely that." I smiled. "But with someone trying to come for you at the club last night, we don't wanna chance it. I don't know what that was about, but these people are really tryin' it like they don't know who the fuck the Pierres or the Baptistes are."

"Same thing I was thinking."

"But, like Nana said. There is always somebody who thinks they're tougher and will try you."

"She ain't never lied," he agreed. "Okay, so eight in the morning now?"

"Yes and the location has changed as well."

"Damn, y'all ain't playing."

"Not at all. We'll also have security there too. So, it's no issues whatsoever. When I say that this is going to be private, it is. Nobody is coming but us, the immediate family—"

"Does yo' mother know?" I asked, like Natacha wasn't my mother.

"Nana had called to give her the information. She didn't answer. I worry about her, especially now."

"Yeah, I stopped by there—"

"Did you?" I frowned. I was definitely shocked to hear it, being that Remy and mom didn't have a relationship at all. Lovely and I did though. She and Lovely were closer, but me and mom shared memories and decent times together here and there.

"Yeah, but she wasn't there. I didn't know she'd been shacking up with that dude. I thought she lived alone."

"Mom been talking to Gary for years now. He's the only one that can deal with her sporadic behavior. One day she's good and, the next, no damn telling."

"So, you talk to her?"

I nodded my head. "Yeah, we talk but not like on a regular but yeah— enough, I guess you can say. She and Lovely were closer with each other though."

"Oh," he said. I could tell he was in thought about that. It was crazy because we didn't get invited in mom's world like that until after you left. I think she felt a void missing once again and she didn't want to lose us too. So, she started reaching out here and there. Like I said, more towards Lovely than me but I got in time too."

"Well— she ain't all bad, I guess."

"No, she's not. She's been hurt in the worst way and, now, it's come back again, but this time with one of her kids. I know it's tough on her. She not answering my calls. She hasn't even talked with Nana, so I know what that means."

"You think she's on drugs again?"

I shrugged. "Probably. I hope not but, with mom, no telling. I've just learned how she is and I deal with her accordingly."

"I see," he said, but I could sense a lil' sadness in his tone.

"You good?"

"Yeah— nawl," he admitted. "I wanted that relationship with mom. I've wanted it for a long time. I just had to come to terms that it would never be. I am glad that y'all have gotten to spend some time with her though. I really thought she was out there just living life in a bubble, to be honest. I guess it's even nice to know that she's with someone too."

"Yeah, and Gary is a good guy. He loves her. She knows it. She don't love him like she loved dad, but she cares for him a lot. She knows he has her back and that's really all that matters to me."

"I feel you," he said with a shake of the head. I didn't know what that was about, but I guess it was his way of processing things.

"So, I think I'm on to something, but I don't wanna speak on it just yet."

"What you mean?"

"People are starting to talk. I don't wanna say nothing yet but, the minute I really find out what's going on, you'll be the first to know."

"So, does this have to do with the dude that got shot at the club? You know we had gone to the hospital before we came here but was told by a nurse that he was still unresponsive. I still don't know who the nigga was but I'm sure the detectives are working on his identity."

"Yeah, and me too," I told him.

"Well, Santana gon' know before all of y'all. He's been on it since early this morning. His name is Corey Cummings and he's from Columbine, Georgia."

I frowned. "That's like two hours away from here."

"Exactly."

"So, he traveled here to try and off you?"

"It seems that way."

"But we don't know that nigga. He definitely don't know us, so who sent him?"

"That's what I wanna know. Who sent his ass because when we find out, he gon' wish he never came?"

"I know that's right," I agreed.

"I'm not ready for tomorrow."

"Me either. It's gon' be hard, that's for sure. I know for Nana it's gon' bring back some really sad feelings and a super harsh reality."

"Definitely is and that's gon' be for all of us."

"I know."

"So, who all is coming?"

"Well, us, of course. Nessa will be there— uh— you don't mind, do you?"

"Oh nawl— I mean, Regan just got here earlier today."

I frowned. "Regan? Is that the girl about my age that you keep going back and forth with?"

"Yeah, that's her ass."

"I thought y'all were off right now."

"We are, but she just popped up here. I didn't even tell her about none of this. Iesha did."

"Why would she do that?"

"Because she thought I'd told her."

"Damn."

"Anyway, she jumped on her father's jet and headed here. So, she'll be there in the morning as well. I don't wanna be rude. Honestly, I don't even have the energy to deal with it."

"I feel you. I don't have the energy to deal with much of nothing my damn self. I really just wanna stay shut in my room, balled up in my bed and not come out for a couple of months."

"I know sis," he said, wrapping his arms around me. I hugged him back, trying my best to hold in the tears as customers entered the restaurant.

"Well, the only other outside person that will be there is Ralph. Of course, at this point, he's family."

"You and Ralph been hanging in there since y'all were in middle school."

I smiled. "I know. We've had our on and off moments, but we always find our way back to each other. Without a doubt, I know he loves me. Hell, I've turned down two proposals." I grinned. "And he's still here."

"That's because you wanna be with him, but the commitment of it all is scary."

"Yeah, and that shit is crazy. I mean, I'm committed to him already, so why am I scared to tie the knot?"

"That could be something dealing with your past and how you've dealt with loss." He shrugged. "Who knows?"

"I can believe it." I nodded.

"So, Fran not coming?"

"Nawl, she said she'd rather cook for the family instead. So, she's opening the restaurant in the morning like nothing is going on, but we're closing at noon. I told her that I would've just closed the place for the whole day, but she insisted on opening, so it don't look suspicious. Especially being that we didn't want nobody to know about the services. Hell, I didn't even tell her that it's been a change of locations. I mean, it's no need. She ain't coming anyway."

"I feel you. How is it to be working with her?"

"It's cool. I mean, we don't always get along. You know Fran loves spending money. She thinks she's the billionaire—"

He laughed.

"I'm serious. But, hey, she works hard for it. I try to tell her to take off sometimes, so she can be with her baby more, but she's been on work mode this past year. Maybe she's saving, so she can always make sure he's good. You know with her broke-down, po' ass family, I'm sure breaking generational curses is at the top of her priority list."

"I forgot Fran had a baby."

"Yeah, he just turned eight months old last month. Cute lil' fella. You know I'm his god-mommy. I think me and Ralph spends more time with him than she does." I grinned a little.

"Well, that's good. I'm surprised you haven't had your own yet."

"Not yet. Until then, he's my baby."

Remy laughed, "I feel you."

"I'm surprised you ain't had none yet."

"Nawl, not yet. I be strapped the fuck up. Listen, condoms on deck, everywhere. I remember me and Nessa was starting the process of having a baby. We'd started taking future steps just in case—" he paused. "But then—well—"

"Yo' ass left. I mean, damn. Left her at the altar like a bad habit."

He regrettably shook his head. "Don't remind me."

"Trust, I know that can be a touchy subject."

"Very touchy, especially when talking to her."

"I'm sure."

"But, anyway," he said, clearly wanting to change the subject. "You okay?"

"Not really, but I will be," I said. However, I highly doubted me being okay would ever be again. I'd lost too much in one lifetime and it was a lot to process. I still hadn't come to terms with losing my aunt and my father, even though I wasn't even born yet. Guess that's why I never was able to come to terms with it. Which could also stem from me not wanting to get married. Crazy, right? But that's how I felt. It was a scary thought because my people were taken way too soon, and it wasn't fair to me or my family. "Well, let me get in here so I can help Fran out. Did you even order your food?"

"Nawl."

"What you wanted?"

"The special of the day with the grape Kool-Aid."

"You still love grape Kool-Aid?" I laughed. "That's all you used to want when we were growing up."

"Yeah, but I ain't had none since I left here. So, I'm looking forward to that."

"Oh, it's good. You gon' be asking for a pitcher like Marla."

We laughed, as I followed him back in the restaurant.

"We'll talk later, sis. Oh, and we're gonna turn up for your birthday before I leave."

"Definitely Bruh. Love you."

"Love you too." He smiled, as I headed for the kitchen.

I entered to see Greta pulling another pan of freshly baked mac and cheese out the oven, as Fran fixed plates. She was one of our other cooks. "Where is Lulu?"

"She's out on the floor helping Amy take orders, since Tanya and Fallon called out."

"Oh, I didn't see her when I walked in," I said. "It is getting packed out there. I know why Tanya's not here, but Fallon said she'd work her shift and then called in actin' sick. I already got word that she was in the club last night, so her ass prolly got a hangover."

"Knowing Fallon, it's true."

We laughed.

"I know and we're closing in two hours, so they better get here within the next hour or they're gonna get turned away."

"I know right," I agreed with Fran.

"Your family's order is over there." Greta pointed.

"Thanks girl. Nana loves herself some of Fran's oxtails. When I told her that was on the menu yesterday, she quickly put in her order then. She sent the cook home after breakfast."

They laughed.

"How is she?" Fran asked.

"She's dealing as best as expected, much like the rest of us."

"I don't even know why you're here," Greta chimed in . "You haven't taken a day since that happened. Well, the day after but that was your birthday. Damn, I still can't believe it." She sighed. "I don't know how you deal."

"It's best I stay busy, ya know. Anytime I'm alone or not actively doing something, it hits me," I admitted.

"Listen, God forbid anything happening like that in my family because if it did, I would be on a leave of absence."

"I don't blame you because I wouldn't be here either," Fran chimed in. "Trust, you would still have your job when you returned."

"She's right." I nodded. "I'm just wired differently. We've been through this a long time ago. Well, technically, I wasn't born until the day after but I'm sure I felt the grief while inside my mom's belly."

"They say babies feel everything the mom's feel. So, I can believe it," Greta said.

"Anyway, this is a tough time for my family. But we'll get through it."

"Yeah, y'all will," Fran said. "Lulu!" she called out, as Lulu entered the kitchen. "Take these drinks out to table five. That's where Remy and the crew are at."

"Okay." She smiled.

"Don't be fuckin' flirting," Fran laughed.

"I'll think about it," Lulu teased.

"Then come back and get their plates."

"Got'cha."

"I'm picking the baby up after work tonight. Where y'all gon' be?"

"We'll be at Nana's," I responded, speaking of me and Ralph. "You may as well let us adopt him," I teased.

"Girl, no. Ralph already asked, and I told him untunt. Have y'all own baby."

I laughed.

"Well, he'll still be in the family since Ralph is your first cousin," Greta chuckled.

"They better have their own baby. My lil' spoiled brat ain't completely leaving my nest."

"It's cool. You got that." I grinned.

I stayed for another thirty minutes, just helping out anywhere I felt needed and then left the restaurant to head home. Ralph was there waiting on me. Honestly, all I wanted was a lil' down time to relax a little because the morning was going to bring about a sad ass day.

After eating dinner with Nana, Josette, Aunt Maddy and Ralph, I headed upstairs to unwind a little. Ralph would be joining me after he returned from walking Fran outside with Lil' D. If we didn't have the memorial service in the morning, he probably would've stayed the night. As of lately, he was always with us. I didn't mind at all. He actually brought a sense joy in my life that I hadn't realized I missed.

I walked in the bathroom and turned on the hot water in the tub. I just wanted to immerse my miseries away. Since house cleaning had already came through and left my bathroom spotless, I didn't have to do any extra cleaning. I grabbed my *7 Chakras Spiritual* bath soak and scooped out enough of the good stuff to put in a tea bag. Once my water was ready, I would toss it in. While relaxing for at least a good twenty-minute soaking, I'd meditatively speak life into my intentions for the week. I lit my *Check Engine Light* Manifestation candle for chakra tuning and alignment. The good Lord knew I needed this shit in my life right about now. When I tell you the *Spiritual Tea Company* had all of my spiritual womanly needs, I didn't have to look any further. I even had Ralph using the products that had been added for the men. He absolutely loved 'em, too.

I looked in the mirror at my reflection staring back at me. I looked drained, tired and just beat from all the senseless shit that had happened within the past week. I was heartbroken, aggravated and over the bullshit. Somebody was clearly gunning for the downfall of my family and, whoever it was, I had a feeling we all knew. Was it a real enemy though or a foe? Either or was scary because of the unknown, but they wouldn't stay hidden forever.

"You good, Babe?"

"Not really love, but I will be."

Ralph wrapped his arms around me. "Yes, you will be," he whispered, softly kissing me in the top of my head.

"How did Lil' D act?"

"You know he put up a fuss."

I grinned. "That's why I didn't wanna walk him out."

"We both knew that. Oh, Fran told me that his father will be keeping him tomorrow."

I frowned while turning off the bath water. "I thought your mom was going to watch him until the service was over."

"Me too, but she said it'll be a change of plans and we can get him back on Tuesday."

I scrunched my nose. I didn't like him staying with just anybody. "Look, I know Marcus is his daddy, but we ain't seen that nigga but a few times. Most of those times was when Fran was pregnant. Yeah, she'll talk about him and say stuff like he stayed to her house with her and Lil' D, but he don't come around like should."

"I agree, but we have to let her raise him how she sees fit. If Marcus wants to step up now, then let him."

"We don't know where that nigga even lives. What if we wanted—"

"Babe, chill out. He'll probably be keeping him at Fran's house. Hell, I'm surprised he ain't moved in that big bitch anyway. The average man would've been took advantage of those living arrangements."

I grinned. "Like you've done by staying here with me."

He playfully smirked. "You know I got my own place. That's yo' ass always wanting me here, so you can be close to Nana."

"I know. I was only teasing you. Nana got this big ass house because she wants us to be near. I just wanna make her happy."

"I know and I just wanna make you happy," he said, as I smiled.

"You're the sweetest man I know."

"I better be." He grinned. "Well, I see you're about to soak, so I'll be waiting for you to come out. I'll find a good movie we can watch until we fall asleep."

"Fix my drink, love. I'll be done in about thirty minutes."

"I'll fix it when you're close to getting out."

"That works too," I told him as he walked out the bathroom, closing the door shut. I took in a deep breath and then tossed my spiritual tea bag in the tub. As I undressed, the only thoughts on my mind was getting to the bottom of this drama. However, the one person I felt knew more than any of us knew was the one person missing. "Mom, where are you?"

ROSELEE "NANA" PIERRE

I sat alone in my bedroom with unpleasant thoughts running endlessly through my mind. I was hurt to the core, and nothing would ever change that. I had just laid two of my babies to rest, but rest would be for eternity. There was a feeling I couldn't explain, and it was far too much for me to deal. However, I knew with God's unwavering grace, I had no choice. I still had family that counted on me. But, how could I be strong for them when I was falling weaker by the day? I did my best to put up a strong front when, inside, I was losing my mind.

Sitting at my vanity staring in the mirror, all I saw was a broken woman. I still had one daughter, but I needed both of 'em. I just knew Natacha would show up to their service, but she didn't. Maybe she was even more lost than I thought she was. How could she not show up to her own daughter's funeral? I could understand she'd lost a lot but, hell, we had too. At some point, she needed to woman the fuck up. I was over it.

"Nana, you good in there?" Royal asked, knocking on my door.

"Yes baby. I'm fine. Just gather everyone in the kitchen to eat. I'm coming," I answered.

"Yes ma'am, but are you sure you're okay?"

"Yes, Royal. I just need a lil' alone time to get myself together."

"Okay," she responded.

I sat, thinking that I really wasn't okay. Out of nowhere, tears began to fall down my face. Just the thought of seeing my family fall apart while standing at the caskets of the children I raised had me mad as hell. I was pissed that someone would do that to them. Lovely didn't deserve to leave here like that. James didn't deserve to die on the anniversary of his mom and dad's tragic ending.

As the tears continued to fall from my eyes, I stood to my feet and picked up the first thing I saw. Without hesitation, I threw the candle straight into the wall. Falling to my knees, I called out for God's favorable mercy. Only a miracle could get me through this. As I wept softly, another tap could be heard at my door. Even though the bedrooms in my house had their own private square footage, I was sure someone had heard the loud noise from me throwing the candle.

"Ma," I heard as my eyes widened. "Mommy, open the door."

Making my way to the door, my heart skipped a beat. I eased it open, almost peeking because I hadn't heard this voice up close and personal in a long time. I smiled inside just to see this lovely face. Even after all the scars, the drugs, the pain, and the absence of not seeing her, Natacha was still one of the most beautiful girls in the world. She reached out and touched my face to dry my tears. It had to be the warmest feeling I'd felt in a long time, literally in years. To see her was to see Nadia again. They were identical twins. Half the time, I still couldn't tell 'em apart.

"Mommy," she let out in that sweet tone that I dearly missed, yet would never forget. She fell in my arms and wept like a baby. I held my daughter as close to my bosom as I could. I just wanted to protect her like I couldn't before. I just wanted to love on her, so she'd know that I was here through whatever and she didn't have to run away again. I just wanted this moment in time to last forever. My heart was full, as we both cried and embraced each other in a way that hadn't happened in twenty-three years.

"It's okay, baby. We got each other and God's got us. It's okay. We're gonna get through this," I consoled her through tears of grief and joy of having her here.

After a bonding period of us relishing in this sweet reality, we finally sat down to talk. I needed to know how she'd been, what her life had been like, and if she was coping with being clean or still indulging in drugs. Ironically, she answered all of my concerns. She even went into her feelings of not being around for years and how it felt to lose her daughter. She was very sad about losing James. She mentioned that he was her favorite nephew and always checked on her to make sure she didn't need anything. She informed me of things that I didn't know, like the close relationship she and Lovely had and how she'd speak with Royal from time to time. When asked why she never really answered my calls or responded to my texts, she simply explained that she couldn't. It was hard for her to talk to me because I made her feel bad for choosing the streets and not us. However, I explained that those were never my intentions. I just wanted her home and, for the first time since tragedy struck, I think she felt the need to be here.

"Did you see Remy when you got here?"

"Yes, and he's so handsome. Reminds me so much of Ramirez. It's amazing how much they favor. It's like he literally spit him out." She grinned a little.

"I know. I say the same thing every time I see him." I smiled. "He has missed you so much."

"I know. He was shocked to see me. Hell, everybody was. It was so good to hug him. I can't lie, at first, he didn't respond well to my affection. I didn't even know how to show it being that it's been so long, but my attempt to show that I cared must've been something he needed—"

"Something he missed."

"Yes, and I could tell by the way he hugged me back. That boy smell so damn good," she teased.

I laughed. This was the bubbly energy I missed about her. She was always the joking one, whereas Nadia was more of the serious one. But they complemented each other in ways that only they understood, but we all felt.

"I know it's been a long time but, after losing Lovely and James, something in me snapped. It's like I woke up from a long twenty-three-year-old nap—"

"More like a damn hibernation."

She grinned. "Yeah, that. But I feel the need to step up. I know you wanna know if this made me wanna go back to using drugs? No, drugs didn't cross my mind. This actually made me madder than it did when Joseph took my twin and my husband. This shit was deep. For one, I knew who took them from us, but not knowing who took James and Lovely don't sit right with me."

"That's how I've felt."

"Don't worry. I'm gonna find out who did this shit, one way or the other."

I regrettably shook my head. "Please, just let the police handle it. I don't want you getting caught up in those streets again."

"Ma, I am the streets, that's what these punks don't know about me. I'm a Pierre; it's certain shit we don't play about, and family is one of 'em."

"Well, you're right about that." I nodded. "I hate you didn't make it to the funeral services. I was looking for you to come."

"I had gone last night after they were transported from the other funeral home to the new location. I listened to y'all's messages and paid my respects privately. I couldn't do it with the family. I needed to be alone with them. It was best that way."

I smiled a little. "I'm just glad that you went. A part of me thought you didn't care. Thought you had gone on a binge—"

"I've been off drugs for a while now. Gary thinks it's only been a year, but it's been way longer than that. I just choose to keep him at bay. I know he loves me, but I'll never love another man like I loved my Ramirez, well, except for Islande."

"Well, they do belong to you and, whether here or gone, that's gonna be forever."

"Definitely," she whispered in a saddened tone.

"So, how you, Ma? You're so worried about everybody else, but are you taking care of yourself? Those children were like your own."

"They were."

"I know you must be going through it and I'm sorry for not being here. You've done so much for me in my presence. I should've been here to help with raising them. I should've did more."

"But you weren't capable."

"I was sick and didn't have the guidance I needed to get through that. It wasn't your fault, though. I don't think nobody could've helped me. Seeing my sister in that casket was something I never thought I could've imagined. I was literally looking at myself laying there. It was a horrific feeling."

"I know, baby."

"That day just keeps playing in my head. I should've never asked Ramirez to go get them. Maybe Joseph wouldn't have lost it to that point. To think I wanted to go. It was times when I felt like I should've against Ramirez's wishes. Then, Joseph would've had to kill us all."

"Don't say that. Don't talk like that."

"It's the truth. It was times when I felt like I should've gone with him, then I'd still be with them."

"But you didn't and you're still here. You still have an opportunity to make this up to us, to your two children who are still here and longing for that love. Just think, Royal never got to experience any of that growing up because you weren't around. She looks at me as Mommy, but she calls me Nana because that's what she was so used to hearing from the older ones."

"I know."

"Remy and Lovely got to experience that good heart of yours and the way you loved them. For them to lose you too in the process of losing their aunt and father, it was devastating."

"I know and I'm sorry. But I'm here now," she said, gently caressing my hand. "I just wanna be a better mother to them and a better aunt to Josette, Lil' Joe and Wesley. They deserve to see the good in me. There is still some good in me, Mommy," she cried. The tears just started streaming down her face. "It's still some good in me, Ma."

"It is baby. I know and I'm glad you can see it now."

We sat comforting each other for as long as we could, until my stomach literally started growling. She looked at me with a jokingly smirk.

"You need to eat lady."

I chuckled. "We both need to eat. Come on. I know they're waiting on us downstairs."

"It smelled so good too when I walked in."

We stood up, as I grabbed her by the hand. "You nervous?"

She nodded her head. "Even though I saw 'em when I came in, I'm really nervous to be sitting at the dinner table with 'em."

"It's not going to be the same either way. Two of 'em are gone."

"Technically, now five of 'em. I still count Joseph. He too was once a good man."

"I agree." I smiled.

Once downstairs, even though the energy was pretty low from just burying James and Lovely, there was still a ray of light shining. Having Natacha back gave us hope in the midst of sadness and grief. It made me feel good to see her and Madeline hug each other. Even though they weren't twins, they still looked a lot alike. It felt good to see the love and warmth that she got from everyone there, especially from Remy. The look on his face wasn't exactly that of love but more so of second chances. I could tell he wanted to give Natacha the opportunity to prove herself, and that's all that mattered. Twenty-three years was a long time to not have someone be in his life but, no matter the length of time lost, he still had mad love for his mother. That would never change.

As the chatter continued around the table, Natacha felt the need to re-introduce her. "For anybody sitting here that may not know me, I'm Natacha, Islande and Royal's mom."

Royal smiled; Remy just sat with a blank expression.

"I've been M.I.A. for a while now."

"James said ever since his parents died. That's been like an eternity ago."

"If eternity is twenty-three years, then James was right. So, who are you?"

"I'm Janet. James' girlfriend."

"Girl, you are not his woman. I am."

"Tasha, don't do that in front of these people. Just because you have the baby out of his five kids don't mean you were his woman."

"Well, you weren't," Tasha shot back.

"Girl, I never claimed to be. I got my bad ass three children by him and that was more than enough. However, James was still my best friend, and I knew he definitely didn't claim you."

"Y'all stop it," Cherry cut in. "We're all his baby mamas. James wasn't committed to nobody. Excuse me, Mrs. Pierre, but James was a hoe. He was for everybody."

"Tuh, just like his grandaddy," I said, as everybody at the table laughed.

"So, who has what with James?" Natacha asked. "He told me about the twins and his three girls, right?"

"Yeah, I have his twin boys right here. Tell your great aunt hey," she said, as they spoke. "And my eight-year-old daughter is also his."

"Yeah, and I have the baby of the bunch. She's four years old, going on twenty-five. She's actually sleeping right now in the next room," Tasha said.

"And I have the seven-year-old," Cherry acknowledged.

"Hey," the little one said.

Natacha smiled. "Hey cutie. Y'all look just like your daddy. The pictures he'd show me do y'all no justice."

"So, you and James were close?" Remy asked with an unsettling frown.

"James had a way of locating me and making sure I was good. We talked," she said. I believed she cut that short, not wanting Remy to feel a way, even though he already was.

"Lil' Joe. You're not so little anymore. It's so good to see your handsome face. You look just like your— dad," she hesitantly said, like she hated to even think about Joseph Sr.

"Aunt Maddy and Nana always tell me that."

"Well, it's true." She smiled. "Who is the beautiful lady with you?"

"This is my woman, Iesha."

"Hi Iesha. Nice to meet you. Do y'all have kids?"

"We do," Iesha responded.

"Twins?"

"Yes, girls."

"Awww, I knew we'd have several sets of twins in our family. The lineage isn't done yet. That comes from me and your mama," she teased.

"I know. Twins just run in our family," Joe responded.

"Sure do since a few generations back. Where are they?"

"They're back home with my mom," Iesha responded. "But you'll meet them soon."

"Great." She grinned. "Josette, where is your little one?"

"Oh, he's with his daddy. I needed a break and a lil' space today," she answered.

"Wesley, you and Gaelle don't have any yet?"

"We're working on it."

Josette rolled her eyes like she couldn't wait for this moment. "I don't know why. You shouldn't want a baby by that slut."

"Josette!" I fussed. "You know better than that."

"What? It's true."

Gaelle looked appalled. "Bae, get yo' cousin before I turn this bitch out."

"Nobody's turning out nothing," Maddy chimed in as she stood up. "Y'all need to chill out. This is not the place for none of y'all's foolishness."

"You're right. If it's anybody here that can't keep their shit together, please leave," I told 'em with a serious stare. Dinner was about to turn into a shit show but not on my damn watch.

Natacha shook her head. "Wow, I'm almost afraid to ask what's going on."

"Please, don't. We'll talk about it later Sis," Maddy said.

"She need to get over it. Nobody's even thinking about that old mess but her," Gaelle said.

"You lucky girl. You lucky," Josette spat.

"Girl, you lucky I don't—"

"Chill out," Wesley cut in. "Josette, when are you gon' let it go? Gaelle and I were on a break, meaning we had broken up. She started talking to Charlie. She didn't know nothing about you and that nigga, and you know it.

It's just easier for you to blame her when, in reality, he was playing you."

"Exactly," Gaelle cut in. "He was talking to both of us. Neither of us knew until you looked through his phone and called me."

"Yeah but, even after that phone call, you still was fuckin' with him."

"That's a damn lie. For one, you had just found out you were pregnant. Why would I do you like that? For two, he wasn't that great in bed anyway," Gaelle bluntly stated, as Wesley shot her the side-eye. "I'm just sayin' Bae. You know what I told you."

"Wow, this is some tv stuff," Fran cut in as she put plates of food on the table.

"Jesus, take the wheel," Natacha blurted out. "This is where all the drama is. The streets ain't got nothing on y'all," she teased. "Who is this handsome fella?"

"I'm Santana—"

"Hopefully, somebody I can get to know better," Fran smirked.

A lil' laughter came from some at the table. "Santana is Remy's best friend," Royal stated.

"Ohhh okay."

"He's a private investigator," Royal added.

"Good, we need you now more than ever."

"I'm working on some leads, don't worry. I'm really good at what I do." Santana smiled with a sincere nod.

"Good. I'm glad to hear that. So, Fran, how have you been? I see you shootin' yo' shot," Natacha joked, as Fran blushed. "I hear you got a lil' baby."

"Yeah, but he's getting bigger by the days though. Royal is his godmother."

"So, I've heard." Natacha approvingly nodded. "Nessa, you're still pretty as ever," she said, making her way around the table.

"Thanks, it's so good to see you."

"Same here. I see life has been good to you."

"Yeah, it's been good," Nessa responded.

"Your club is doing great."

I frowned.

"Mama, just because I haven't been around don't mean I don't know what's going on here."

"Nobody even see you like that," Maddy chimed in.

"I know how to roam the streets on the low. I've even been inside your club one night. It's really nice in there. Some upscale shit."

"Oh wow. I didn't know."

"I know." Natacha smiled. "I always thought you and Islande would be together forever."

Nessa looked over at Remy. "Yeah, me too." She shrugged. "I guess things don't always work out as planned."

"It's never too late though," Natacha said. "But, hey, I'm sorry. Excuse me," she said to the young lady that none of us really knew. "Islande sitting here with someone new. Do you care to introduce me, son? I would like to know more of what's been going on in your life."

"Not really," Remy uncaringly responded.

"Yeah Remy, who is she?" Josette asked with her loud country mouth. I was sure she was trying to get the attention off of her, especially since Gaelle told the world that her man's sex game was wack. I mean, seriously, I couldn't make this shit up.

"I'm Regan," the young lady said, standing up like it was a cause for all that. "I guess you can say that Islande is my man. We've been together for a number of years; sometimes we're on and, then, others well, we take a break from time to time," she admitted.

"No, don't do that. You know we are not in a relationship right now and won't be getting back together."

"So, why she come to the funeral? We thought y'all were a couple," Josette said.

"She came because she flew here from New Hampshire and wanted to be here for me. I don't believe nothing was wrong with that. Anything else you wanna ask Josette?"

"Remy, I was only asking what everybody else was thinking," she responded.

"You need to be more concerned about yo' man out here giving out Vienna snacks for dinner," Gaelle snuck in.

"Oh wow," Josette said, standing up like she was about to start swinging at any given second.

"Sit yo' ass down," Maddy jumped in. "Y'all two gon' have to stop this shit and I mean right damn now!"

"Yes ma'am," Gaelle softly said with a cheeky smirk. I believe that was all the get back she needed for Josette.

Josette sat back down. "I'm over it. I'm gon' let you have that."

"Thank you," I said. "Because this ain't it y'all. We're family. We all we got left and we need to do better."

"I agree Ma," Maddy said. "I'm glad you're here sis. Your presence has been missed for a long time. You look good."

"Considering the circumstances, I feel good just being around y'all. I know I can't say this enough, but I'm sorry for not being here over the years. Royal, you're a beautiful young lady with brain and wits. I know we speak every now and then, but I need you to know that I love you. I have so much making up to do with you and, if you allow me to, I would love to be a part of your life now. Granted, I'm very grateful for Ma raising you. She done a wonderful job."

Royal simply looked over at me with a smile. "She did and I'll forever love her for that."

"I don't expect things to go back to normal. We really don't have a normal, not anymore, but give me a chance. Please, I need you and Islande to just give me a chance."

Neither said nothing in response to that. I believed they were waiting for the other to speak up, no telling.

After an awkward silence, Natacha continued. "Well, let's eat. I'm hungry. Plus, Ma's stomach was growling like crazy upstairs," she joked to lighten the heavy energy in the room.

"Yeah, let's eat," Wesley chimed in.

As we all began to dig in and feast on the delicious food that Royal had prepared, Natacha sent shockwaves around the table. "Nessa, how's your son?"

Remy damn near choked off his grape Kool-Aid, as Natacha aggressively patted him on the back. "Son? Nessa you got a son?! When the hell did that happen?!"

ISLAND "REMY" PIERRE

"Islande, lower yo' fuckin' voice. I know you see everybody standing at the window watching and listening."

"You think I care about that?" I pondered as I paced the grounds in the backyard. I glanced up at the window to see Nana trying to back away quickly, like I didn't see them being nosey. I just shook my head and directed my attention back to Nessa. "I wanna know why you didn't tell me you had a baby."

"First off, it's none of your business. Second thought, we don't even talk like that. This the first time I've seen or spoke with you since you left me ten years ago."

I looked at her with a menacing stare. I was heated after hearing that shit. She could've just told me she had a son. For her not to had me thinking, why the hell not?

"Why the hell not, Nessa? Why you ain't just tell me?"

"What was that going to change? You've been here for a week, and you expect me to just open up about every little detail of my life?! Had you kept yo' ass around or took me with you, then I wouldn't have to tell you nothing. You'd already know."

"That don't matter. We're talking about a baby, a kid? I mean, damn. How old is he?"

"He's three years old. Anything else you wanna know?"

I stood speechless. Never did I think she'd have a baby and, if she did, I didn't think I'd care this much. "How?"

"How what Islande?" she impatiently asked.

"You know what I mean, damn!"

Nessa irritably shook her head. "I don't understand why you so mad. Me having a child isn't your concern, nor should it matter. Why are you making this a bigger deal than what it should be?"

"Because you got a whole kid out here and ain't bothered to say nothing since I've been home."

"Would it matter any?"

"Huh?"

"Huh?" she mocked back with her nose scrunched up. "You heard me."

"I don't know what you mean by that, but I would've liked to know. I mean, you had three miscarriages because you couldn't carry our babies no further than two to three months, then suddenly you have a three-year-old."

"It wasn't suddenly and, again, it don't matter."

"Fuck!" I let out. I couldn't understand why I was so pissed, but I was. I loved this woman and, when we were together, we tried to have a baby more than once. We both felt children would've really made our lil' family whole. I wanted kids so bad and not just by anybody but by her. I knew we could give our children the love that my parents weren't here to give me. I couldn't lie; a part of me felt hurt to know that she'd had a baby on me. "Is it rent-a-cop's?"

"Who, Darnell?"

"Don't play with me, Nessa. You know who the hell rent-a-cop is."

"No."

"No what?"

"No, he's not his."

"Well—" I paused, tryna get my thoughts together. "So, you was giving it up like that?"

She angrily scowled. "Nigga, if yo' people wasn't still peepin' out that window, I would slap the hell outta you!"

I grabbed her by the arm. "Who—"

"Islande, turn her arm loose," Natacha demanded as she stepped outside.

I really didn't care about her coming to Nessa's rescue, but it was something about the tone of her voice that took me back to when I was a kid getting fussed at. I let Nessa's arm go.

"I'm sorry Nessa. You can go back inside. Lemme have a private talk with my son, please."

"Okay," Nessa said. She didn't waste any time going back in the house.

I looked over at Natacha with a short-tempered stare. "Why you come out here interrupting us?"

"Because things were getting a lil' too physical."

"You the one started it."

"I didn't know you didn't know."

"Well, as you can I see, I didn't. But how you knew she had a baby?"

"Islande, this might be a big city, but it's small to us. Everybody knows everybody, damn near. I really didn't come out til night, but I kept my ears to the streets. I knew shit. I'd heard shit. I knew. It ain't like he's a newborn. He's been here for a couple of years or so now."

"Have you seen him?"

"No, she protects him from the outside world."

"Meaning."

"She's not showcasing him or anything, not around these parts of the city. They come out I imagine but, for the most part, she shops where she lives which is on the outskirts of the city."

"Yeah, I've been there," I said, now thinking this was why she didn't want me to come in her house. Maybe it was toys lying around or pictures in sight. "So, you know who the daddy is? Did you even see her pregnant?"

"I never saw her pregnant, but I don't see much of Nessa anyway. And about the father— I don't have a clue, honestly. I think that's a conversation between you and her."

"What you think I was doing before you showed up?"

"Yeah, but you were doing a lil' more than talkin'. You should never put your hands on a lady like that."

"I know but I wasn't hurting her. I just wanted answers."

"But, why, son?"

I glanced down at the ground and then up at the sky. I just needed answers. I hated being left out of the loop when everybody else knew. "I'm just upset that nobody told me, not even Nana."

"Why though?" she asked again.

"Because—"

"Because what?"

"Because I still love her," I unexpectedly admitted.

Natacha frowned. "You still love her after you've been gone for ten years?"

"You still love us, right? Or is that all a front?" I had asked before I even realized it.

"Touché," she uttered. "Of course, I still love y'all. I'm your mother. I'll always love you."

"You had a helluva way of showing it."

"Okay, I deserved that."

"What made you turn up now, anyway? You didn't even come to your own daughter's funeral, yet now you're here asking for second chances. What kind of shit is this?"

"You're wrong about one thing. I paid my respects last night at the funeral home. I sat with my child all night and didn't leave until six this morning. I talked to her and James until I had no words left. I'm broken over this shit, but the difference is that I'm not letting it take me out like it did before. If anything, it woke me up."

"You sholl was sleep for a long time."

She snickered a little. "Same thing yo' grandma said. Look, I don't expect you to believe in me. I don't even expect you to forgive me, but I would like for you to know that I'm here for you now. Now may be too late for you, but I ain't going nowhere."

"Yeah, I hear you," I said, not really in the mood for any of this. It was hard taking the word of a woman that left us behind and didn't care to look back. For some reason, seeing her felt good but that was about it. She had showed up too late in my life to expect anything out of me. I'd give and show her respect but nothing more. Nana once told me that even a dog was due respect, and she did mean way more to me than a damn dog. So, she could have that.

"You okay?"

"Not really," I responded. "It's like it's one thing after another. I'm still trying to find out what happened to Lovely and James. On top of needing to know why that nigga wanted to kill me. Then, I hear about Nessa having a child—damn. I should just pack up and fly back. If I stick around too long, I'm gon' end up killing a bitch."

"Well, so you know— I've been told that the Cannons are behind this."

I looked over at her with curious eyes. "You heard that?"

"I know it to be true. I just don't understand the reason behind it unless Rod was involved. No telling what kind of feelings have been festering since you killed Rudy. They took it really hard, especially Tony. Rod was never really involved in their mess. But who really knows what's going through a man's mind? Maybe this was his way of getting close to Lovely, only to take her out. I mean, look at the timing of it all. Whomever did this wanted us to relive what happened twenty-three years ago. They were cold with it ,which means that retaliation has to be fuckin' North Pole cold too. Fuck the police and their piss po' ass job of handling this shit."

I stared at her. The look in her eyes meant business. "So, you think that pussy ass nigga was behind this?"

"Had to be. Why else was Lovely the one that had gotten hit so many times? It seemed like she was the target. Either her or James, but my gut is telling me it was her. James could've easily been dealt with. He kept his ass in the streets. You know him. He wasn't scared of nobody, but somebody caught them off guard. Lovely always carried her gun, not that I would've thought she'd ever need it, but I'm sure she would've fired back if she had the chance. They didn't give her a chance," she said through a painful tone. "They killed my child and the baby she was carrying," she said as the tears fell from her eyes.

At that moment, I felt bad for her. I could see she was hurt, the devastation showed in her eyes, and it reminded me of that same look years ago. It wasn't until now that I could remember just how much losing auntie and dad did to her. However, she masked it a lil' better because now, she was stronger than before. She wanted to take charge and do something about it rather than wallow in her sorrows. She sounded like a woman on a mission, and I was going to have her front and back to find out who did this.

"I think the first thing we need to do is to catch Rod slipping. Since this shit happened, he's been looking over his shoulders."

"How you know?"

"I've been lowkey watching his ass."

"Oh okay," I said, realizing just how much she was invested in this. "So, what have you determined?"

"Well, he's home most times. He stepped out on his porch the other morning, seemingly talking to himself— maybe even God, who knows? He could've even been talkin' to her—"

"Lovely?"

"Yeah— who knows?"

"You're right. No telling— but how did he seem to you?"

"Strangely, he seems hurt. When he was out on the porch, he cried out. It was just a loud holler, sounded pretty painful to me. Then, he went to the funeral home. I'm guessing to try and see her but, of course, they didn't let him."

"Which one?"

"The one where they moved their bodies to."

"That is strange because nobody knew about the location move but us."

"Which tells me that someone on the inside is talking to him or maybe he was there to watch the move?" she pondered.

"I don't know. Something about this whole thing is off to me. The guy that's in the hospital isn't even from here but, I believe once we find out who he's connected to, things will start to come together."

"What about your lil' private detective friend?"

"He's on it. He did get a name and where he's from," I said, just as my cell phone rang. I glanced down at the number; it wasn't saved but it was a local Gainesboro area code. "Hold on," I said while answering the phone. "Hello."

"Hello, is this Islande Pierre?"

"Yes."

"This is Detective Lewis."

"Any information?"

"Not really, however, I thought you would've wanted to know this. The young man that was in the hospital has died from his injuries."

My eyes widened. "He's dead?"

"Yes, he died about an hour ago."

"Wow," I uttered. "So, you haven't found anything else out yet?"

"Not yet, but we definitely have leads since we found out who he was. I'll let you know the minute we find out something of importance."

"Okay, thank you."

"You're welcome."

The call ended, as I looked over at Natacha. "The dude in the hospital died."

"Good, two down and few others to go," she uncaringly boasted.

"What you mean, two down?"

"Remember the name Stoney Harris?"

I frowned, now having to think back because the name certainly rang a bell. "Stoney Harris?" I repeated. "Oh, the guy that I was questioned about? The one that got killed a couple of nights after Lovely and James?"

"Yeah."

"What about him? From what I'm told, he ain't have nothing to do with it."

"Well, right now, I don't know who all was involved. However, I knew he had it in for my nephew because James told me. So, yeah, he had to go."

My eyes stretched. "Wow. That was you? You did that?"

"Yeah, and I'm not done. Anybody that had something to do with this is going straight to hell with gasoline drawls on. I'm not resting until all dem muthafuckas dead."

I sat at the desk inside my suite, just needing the break from all the bullshit. The dinner that was supposed to be a family gathering of love turned out to be all but that. The drama seemed never ending. Hell, I still didn't understand most of it. Josette and Gaelle were on some other shit. They were going back and forth over a nigga that Gaelle ain't even with. I couldn't even understand why

Josette was still with him. I guess that wasn't my problem though. I had enough shit on my mind.

Natacha showing up was definitely something I wasn't expecting. I didn't even think I'd get the chance to see her while I was here. She had a real smooth way of dodging people and staying hidden in plain sight. I couldn't understand that part for shit. After all those years, it was a part of me that felt some sense of comfort when it was just me and her talking, yet I still was confused by all of it.

Then Nessa— damn, talk about the element of surprise. I wasn't ready for that shit.

"Why aren't you coming to bed?" Regan asked as she joined me.

"I'm not sleepy. I have a lot on my mind."

"Like what? That girl and her baby."

"That girl happens to be a woman, but yeah— that and other stuff."

"But that's the main thing on your mind."

"Does it fuckin' matter if it is?"

"Yeah, it matters. Here I am showing up hoping that we can reconcile, but you're here thinking 'bout another bitch that has clearly moved on."

I shot her ass the side-eye. I didn't like that *bitch* shit.

"Hell, I had moved on too. I was the one that left her—"

"So, why you in your feelings? If you left her, then you should be okay with her having a baby. What you think? Life didn't stop just because you moved away."

"Whatever."

"And your mama, the woman that rose from the dead was so disrespectful. She was talking to that girl like I wasn't sitting beside you."

"My mama don't know you—"

"Hell, she don't know you either," she sassed. "Like I said, she still could've shown me a lil' more respect than that."

"Nobody owes you shit. Who the hell you think you are to come around my family and expect them to lift you up when they're down or to even respect you?"

"I'm apparently more than them country bumpkins sitting at that table. All except your Nana," she eased in like that was supposed to make what she'd said better.

I grinned a little. That was my way of not spazzing out on her ass. "So, you calling my family country bumpkins, but you expect me to wanna be with you?"

"I didn't call you that. I said they were. I can see why you moved away. I would've too if I were you."

"Wow, they weren't the reason I moved away. I can't believe yo' bird brain ass would think that. I love my family, everything about them. I moved for personal reasons but, if it weren't for that, I would've never left here."

"And you'd be broke and unhappy," she said, as I frowned a little.

"First off, does it look like my family is broke? You sat at the table inside of my Nana's seven-thousand square foot home. You saw the cars parked in the driveway. My Nana has a cook, house cleaners and all. Her bank account is nice as fuck. My sister owns a known restaurant in town. The woman that cooked the food for us is the head cook at the restaurant. My aunt runs a multi-million-dollar online women's boutique. Wesley has his own empire—"

"Okay, I get it. But, let's be real. They got all that because of you."

"You a damn lie. They got that because of them."

"Yeah, whatever Islande. I think we should just go back tomorrow."

"Huh?" I scowled.

"Huh?" she retorted. "You heard me."

"No, I think you should just go back tomorrow. I don't even know why you're here."

"I don't either because it's apparent you don't want me here."

"You finally said something that I can agree with. Please, pack yo' shit and haul ass."

"Wow— you act like I can't snap a finger and have my father's jet here in no time. I don't need your ass," she said as a knock sounded off at the door. "Glad, I'm leaving; I don't like Santana's ass anyway."

"Well, that feeling is mutual." I walked to the door. Santana couldn't have showed up at a better time. Hopefully, she'd fly her boujee ass out tonight. I was over her anyway.

I gathered my composure before opening the door. I didn't even want him to know that we'd just had it out over some stupid shit. All he was gon' say was that *I told you so*, and I ain't wanna hear it. He never cared for Regan. He felt she was only with me because of the money and not that she needed it, but that it complemented her spoiled wealthy ass. I opened the door, totally surprised by who was standing there.

With an uncertain expression on my face, I asked, "What brings you here this time of night?"

"I think we need to talk."

"Oh, I think we did enough talking for the day."

"You're still so fuckin' bullheaded—"

"I'm bullheaded and you're fuckin' secretive."

"Secretive? Nigga, how am I holding secrets when yo' ass ain't been around to tell 'em to you? It's been ten years. I really didn't think you were ever coming back. I'd ask about you from time to time when talking to Mrs. Pierre—"

"And when you started calling her that? She was always Nana to you, too."

"Yeah, until her beloved child up and left me. I then felt I wasn't part of the family no more. So, I started acting like it."

"You are so full of shit."

"Take it how you want. She understood when I explained it to her, so get over it."

"Here I was thinking it was Santana but, damn, it's worse," Regan sassed as she walked up front, luggage in tow.

"I forgot she was with you," Nessa said with a slick roll of the eyes.

"How the hell did you forget that? You just showed up here to test me."

"Regan, please, chill out," I said.

"No, let her keep going and watch what happens to her high-dollar ass."

"Listen girl, don't let the expensive brands and pretty face fool you. I can get ratchet if need be."

I smacked my lips. I didn't know what her definition of ratchet was, but Ian think she wanted no parts of Nessa.

"Y'all just chill out."

"Nah, that's yo' bitch getting in convo that don't involve her."

"Why you here?" Regan asked with an attitude.

"From the looks of things, you're leaving, so what's it to you?"

I just shook my head, as if the fuckin' day wasn't already filled with enough drama.

"Oh, I'm leaving sweetie. You want his ass, you can have him."

"You can't give me somebody that don't even want you."

At that time, Regan charged Nessa's way and, as I grabbed her, Nessa snuck in a quick open hand slap to Regan's face.

"Yooo!" Santana said as he showed up just in time to help me stop this foolishness.

"You gon' let that bitch hit me and get away with it?"

"You was the one that lunged at her first Regan. Calm down," I insisted, as she started kicking and swinging in the air.

"I wish you would touch me," Nessa spat, as Santana stood between her and the wild licks being thrown their way. "I don't have time for this. I'm leaving."

"No bitch, come back. You wanna slap me? Slap me when no one is holding me."

"Princess, you don't want this. Go home," Nessa coolly said as she snatched away from Santana and walked off.

"Turn me loose," Regan spat, as Santana closed the door shut.

"Regan, I don't believe you want no parts of her. That's a real country girl—"

"Fuck you, Santana."

I grinned to myself. Him saying that was the real highlight of the night.

"If she's still outside by the time I make it out there, it's gon' be some smoke in this dirty muthafuckin' city."

I couldn't even hold it no more. I began to laugh.

"What's so fuckin' funny?" she snarled.

"Oh nothing— I just ain't never seen you so 'bout it 'bout it."

Santana laughed.

"I'm just saying."

"Hush Islande. Your fuckin' sarcasm is not cute! I'm leaving. I have a jet waiting on me."

"Fine," I said, looking back at Santana who was standing in front of the door. "Let her leave."

"You and I are done, Islande."

"I hope you meant that" I responded.

"Move Santana!"

"With pleasure." He grinned, as she wasted no time dragging her luggage behind and making her exit.

I just looked over at my good ole buddy with a shake of the head. "Just when I thought it couldn't get no worse, it did."

VANESSA "NESSA" LUCAS

I woke up with a banging headache, as I looked over on my nightstand to see the damn near empty bottle of Armand de Brignac Ace of Spades Champagne staring back at me. "Muthafucka," I groaned, just as my cell phone began to ring.

Rolling over, I answered, "Hello."

"Well, damn. What kinda night you had?"

"Good morning to you too, Mama."

"Hey girl," she said with sarcasm. "Long night? Did you go over to talk with Islande like I suggested you do?"

"Yes, but—"

"Don't tell me you chickened out."

"I didn't even have a chance to speak with him because that lady was there."

"Talkin' 'bout the one that was at Roselee's house?"

"Yep, and her mouth so reckless, she was about to get her ass beat."

"What the hell?"

"You heard me right. She started talkin' shit the second she saw me at the door. I don't even know who she is, but she was about to be eatin' a knuckle sandwich playing with me."

Mama laughed. "I know damn that woman wasn't startin' no shit."

"Yes, she was. But she was mad already anyway. It looked like Islande was putting her out." I grinned.

"Well, you did say that he told everybody at the table in front of her that they weren't together."

"And did," I laughed. "Anyway, she was definitely leaving because she told me that I could have his ass."

"How she give away a man that don't want her?"

I busted out laughing. "That's exactly what I asked her."

"She apparently wasn't ready for you."

"She tried it though and ended up getting slapped."

"Damn. You slapped her?"

"Slapped the shit out her."

Mama laughed. "She ain't know you was crazy."

I laughed. "Right. Anyway, what is Mir doing?"

"He's still sleeping but, when he wakes up, I'm gonna bring him home. He's been askin' 'bout you."

"I know. I miss my baby. I appreciate you keeping him for me. I know you usually keep him on the weekends anyway because I be at the club, but yesterday was tough. Thanks for having my back as always."

"You know this my baby, too. I'll keep him whenever you need me too."

"You're like his daddy and I'm the mama."

Mama laughed. "I be damn. I must be the mama and yo' ass is the daddy. Ion look like no damn man."

I laughed out loud. "Me either."

"He is a lil' miracle baby."

I smiled. "He really is. My lil' preemie."

"His bad ass ain't no preemie no more. Fat ass," Mama teased.

"Don't do my baby, woman."

"No, but seriously, you gotta have that talk with Islande and, the sooner, the better."

"I don't know why everybody's so pressed about me talking to him. He ain't Mir's father."

"You sound like a fool. You done said that shit so much, you startin' to believe it yo' damn self."

"Well, he ain't."

"You used his sperm, so how the fuck?"

"Yeah, but—"

"Ain't no buts, Nessa. You always said if he came back home, you'd tell him and, now, he's home."

"Yeah, but he didn't come back for me. He came back for other reasons."

"Don't matter. He's still home and that's all that counts. Mir needs to know his father. I know it won't be easy, but he deserves to know. I don't plan on being his daddy forever," she grinned.

"You said you would."

"Stop playing with me. That man deserves to know."

"And I'll tell him when the time is right. Until then, chill out woman."

"Mir knows him anyway."

"How the hell?" I scowled.

"I've been showing him pictures of his daddy since he turned one."

"Wow, why you didn't tell me that? Mir has been asking me where his daddy pictures at and I never knew what he was talking about. You dirty for that."

"Well, you wouldn't have showed him."

"What if Islande wouldn't have come, then what?"

"Then, I'd still be telling you to call that man, that's what."

"A'ight mama. I can't win with you. Again, I'll tell him soon enough."

"You better or I will. He needs to know before he leaves."

"Okay," I irritably groaned. "I need to shower now. I got a headache."

"I'll be over at some point."

"Okay."

We ended the call as I sat up in bed, rubbing my eyes. Mama really had a way of irritating me with this *tell Islande* bullshit. I slid out of bed and headed into the bathroom. I just needed a really soothing, hot shower. But, first, I needed to brush my teeth. Morning-after, liquor breath was no joke. After brushing up, I turned on the shower water and took off my night shirt. I stepped under the steaming water and let it pour all over my body. This was always one of the best feelings ever. Sitting on the shower bench, I allowed the water to sprinkle all over, from my head down to my toes. I grabbed the *Spring Fling Lush Body Wash*, poured a little on my bath sponge and began to lather up. The smell was intoxicating. *The Spiritual Tea Company* had done it again. This was exactly what I needed to take the edge off.

Thoughts of Islande began to flood my mind. A part of me felt bad for moving the way I did, but I had my reasons. If ever I was going to have a baby, it was going to be by him. We'd gone through procedures even back then to freeze his sperm, and to preserve my eggs just in case I would need a surrogate later. Being that I was so young, the possibility of me carrying wasn't likely due to the number of miscarriages I'd already had by him. Then, he left me, not knowing that I was pregnant for the fourth time. I wasn't going to tell him til that night after we'd gotten married, but I didn't have the chance to. He ghosted me and never looked back. I was heartbroken, but a part of me still loved him til this day.

By mama working as a custodian at a fertility clinic, she was the one that suggested that we freeze Islande's sperm too, for *just in case* purposes. I never intended on using it after he left me like that, but baby fever kicked in three years ago and I figured I'd give it another try. This time with technology being on the rise and seeking the help from the top OBGYN specialists around, I did the unthinkable. I held a baby longer than anyone ever expected. It was only three things I got out of bed for and that was to pee, shit and shower. Three years later, I gave birth at twenty-seven weeks pregnant. My lil' miracle baby was only two pounds at birth. Luckily, his organs were already developed, but he still had to spend months in NICU. Now, he was healthier than ever, functioning at the rate he should've been and some, and smarter than a fifth grader. At least that's the way it seemed with his lil' nosey butt.

Once out the shower, I dried off and headed into my bedroom to find something to throw on. After having had a drama filled last couple of days, all I wanted was to lie on my sectional and watch episodes of The Walking Dead until I caught up. However, Mir would be coming home, so I'd probably end up watching Despicable Me parts 1,2 and 3 instead.

As I searched my closet for something comfortable to throw on, I was startled by Darnell walking up behind me.

"Shit! You scared me."

"My bad, I thought you heard me come in."

"I honestly was so zoned out, I didn't even hear the alarm sound off."

"What you doing?"

"Trying to find something to put on. You off today?"

"Yeah, and I'm glad. Figured I'd spend the day with you and Mir. Where is he?"

"Still with his gammy. She's bringing him home whenever he wakes up though."

"Oh, okay," he said, as I walked out the closet while slipping a sundress on. I could tell he was a lil' irritated by his stance, even though he tried to play it off.

"What's wrong with you?"

"Nothing."

I shook my head. "You a nothing lie."

He shrugged, still looking like he wanted to talk a lil' shit.

"Come on with it," I urged to get the shit over with.

"Where were you last night? I see you had a good time," he said, looking at the champagne on my nightstand.

"Yeah, by myself."

He frowned like he didn't believe me. "You sure about that?"

"Oh, you think I'd be laid up in here with another nigga while yo' ass got a key?"

"What that mean?"

"Means you can walk up in my house at any given time, so why would I be so dumb to do that?"

"Well, I called you last night and text, but you didn't respond or call back. So, what were you doing besides getting hammered?"

"I got your phone call and meant to call you back, but it simply slipped my mind. Plus, you only called once, so it couldn't have been that important."

"I figured I'd give you the space you needed to do whatever you were doing."

"Ion like how you insinuating shit. If you got something to say, just say it, Darnell."

"Were you with that nigga?"

I sat on the side of the bed. Having to confess I'd gone to the room to see Islande was one thing but, damn, I felt like I needed to say more.

"Well—"

"I wasn't with him."

"Where were you?"

"I—uh—I did go to the hotel because I felt like we needed to talk about the conversation that wasn't finished—uh— earlier that day."

He frowned. "What conversation Nessa?"

"He found out I had a baby—"

"What you mean he found out? He never knew you had a kid?"

"How was he supposed to know? I never told him."

"So, none of his people ever told him you had a baby?"

"No, I guess not. So, when his mom mentioned it-"

"Hold up— his mom? Where she come from?"

"Listen nigga. Do you wanna know what I have to say or nah? It don't matter where she came from. Ain't she family? Whether she been around or not, she's still family."

"Ok, you got a point," he said, brushing that off. "Carry on because I thought he would've known about Mir. So, what was the big deal that you had to go to his hotel room to finish telling him you had a child?"

"Well, for one, he made a big deal out of it. He didn't know and that bothered him. Things got a lil' heated between us and that's when his mama stepped in."

"What you mean heated? Why is he getting upset about something that has nothing to do with him? He act like he's not over you. Is that what this is really about?"

"No, I wouldn't necessarily say that. I'm just sayin'—"

"Sayin' what, Nessa?"

"I just felt like we needed to finish that conversation. Maybe I did owe him an explanation."

"After ten years of him leaving you behind, I don't think you owe him shit. What is wrong with you? He's not Mir's father. You were intrauterine inseminated. Hell, I would like to someday adopt him and raise him as my own."

"Well, that's gonna be a problem," I said with hesitation.

He unpleasantly frowned. "Why is that? When we started dating a little over a year ago, that was something we discussed. Has it changed since that nigga came back?"

"It's not that simple."

"What you mean by that? I'm over this evasive talk. Just say what's on your mind. Are you still in love with him?"

At that moment, I felt cornered. Kind of like I just wanted to walk out and leave the shit alone.

"So, you can't answer me, Nessa? Are you still in love with that nigga?"

"No," I answered.

"Okay, so what's the fuckin' problem?"

I paced in circles trying to make sure my words came out right. "Well—um—"

"What Nessa?! Spit it out!"

"He's Amir's father!" I yelled.

Darnell's eyes stretched wide as hell as he looked at me with confusion written all over his face. "Say what now?"

"Darnell—"

"No, what did you say Nessa?"

"Islande is Amir's father."

Darnell plopped down on the bed, almost like he'd lost the battle and was done for. He gazed over at me with a look of disappointment, yet clueless and lost. "How?"

"Huh?"

"How is he the father? Did you sleep with him but acted like you'd gotten a procedure done?"

"No."

"Well, how is that possible?"

"I used his sperm, his uh— his frozen sperm."

Darnell stood up, sat back down, then stood back up. The nigga was befuddled like a muthafucka, and I couldn't blame him. If I had just gotten a whiff of some news like that, I'd probably be dazed as hell too.

"Wow, so how did you get his sperm?"

"Islande's sperm has been at the fertility clinic since before he left ten years ago. I wanted a baby and I wanted one bad, so I decided to use it. We'd signed paperwork years ago. It was nothing, rather fairly easy to get it done without him being here— or without him even knowing."

"I'm confused." He said, scratching his head. "So, if he don't know, why tell him now?"

I shrugged as I saw the hurt in his eyes. "Because it's the right thing to do Darnell."

"If you tell him this, it will be the end of me and you."

"So, you're breaking up with me?"

"If he finds out that Amir is his son then, yes, this relationship is over."

I stood in silence, just pondering over my thoughts before I spoke. I really had grown to love Darnell and would hate for us to end like this, so it was quite natural to struggle with what I needed to do versus what I wished I could do. But, then, reality hit me, and I found myself having no choice but to— "I'm so sorry," I said as tears began to well in the corners of my eyes. "I have to tell him."

Once those words escaped my lips, Darnell looked at me with a quaint but saddened smile, as the curve in his lips trembled a bit. It was almost like he knew it was the end anyway. "I wish you the best with that situation Nessa." After saying that, he walked out the bedroom and didn't bother coming back.

"So, girl, where he went?"

I looked over at Shakita with a shake of the head. "I have no fuckin' clue. He's off today, so no telling. I just hope he don't run into Islande. That shit might turn out real bad."

"I know that's right. Chile and, the way Islande turned out the club Saturday night, that nigga still got it. Just as crazy as ever," she added. "But are you gonna tell him for real, though?"

I nodded my head. "Yeah, I think I am."

"You can't be thinking girl. You gotta be for sure."

"I'm gonna tell him," I said, pouring me a shot of Remy 1738.

"Fix me one of dem."

"I got you." I poured her a shot and handed over the shot glass. "I'm just gonna ask him to come back over. I don't wanna go back to that hotel room. Crazy ass girl might still be there and I ain't tryna go to jail."

"You should've beat her ass."

I laughed. "Yeah, I really should've. I don't see how Islande dated her. She's so boujee, like she's entitled or something. He was always so down to earth. Those type of women turned him off—"

"Yeah, that was the nigga you used to know. No telling if all that money has changed him."

"Nawl, we talked about that. He's still the same when it comes to what he likes and how he deals. She just had to be a consistent, good piece of pussy."

Shakita laughed. "Could've been, who knows?"

"Right, but I don't wanna run into her again. I'm telling you, I won't be able to control myself. Plus, she look like the type that'll call the police on my ass," I laughed.

"Yeah, well— stay away from her. Ain't nobody got time for that."

"So, how do you think Islande will feel once he learns the truth?"

"Oh, he'll be mad at first but only because you're just telling him, but he'll get over it. I'm positive."

"I can't believe it's come to this. Hell, if I'd known he'd be coming home this soon— I would've just fucked him and gotten pregnant instead," I joked.

"Girl, you stupid," Shakita laughed.

"Mama agreed to help me with Mir but, this whole time, she's said that I needed to tell Islande. The promise I made was if he ever came home, I'd tell him."

"Well, he's home."

I looked over at Shakita with a slick roll of the eyes. "Duh, bitch."

She laughed, "I'm just sayin'."

"I never thought past him showing up here nor did I ever think past Mir asking for his dad. I just knew I wanted my baby by him and by any means necessary."

"Well, you made that happen, that's for sure."

"Now, I'm faced with having to tell him. Mama just confessed that she's been showing Mir pictures of him ever since he was a year old. So, I'm sure he knows his face. But with Darnell being in his life, I don't think he's put much thought in it. I mean, Mir is smart, so it's hard to know what all he's truly comprehending."

"You're right about that. His lil' ass is definitely smart. He asked me the other day was my hair a wig or my hair."

I busted out laughing. "That's cause I be pulling my wig off around him and he be laughing like it's funny. Girl, that lil' boy is a mess."

Shakita laughed. "I just looked at him cause he was staring at me so serious with those big pretty eyes of his. I mean, he really wanted to know. I'm like, *Mir, it's my real hair. Pull it.* Girl, he said, *I believe you.*"

We fell out laughing.

"I told you, he's a mess!"

"Like, I don't know it," she chuckled. "Anyway, you may as well hit him up."

I glanced down at my cell phone while taking another shot. "Okay, fuck it," I said while calling him. I looked over at Shakita with mixed emotions. I didn't know how this was about to go, but I sure as hell was about to find out. I shrugged. The phone rang a couple of times, then went to voicemail. "It went to voicemail."

"Like, he sent you to voicemail or it just rang until it went there?"

I shrugged again. "I think he sent me to voicemail."

"Damn, call back."

"Okay," I said, calling him back. This time on the first ring, it went to voicemail. "Oh, this nigga sending me to voicemail."

"Oh, he big mad," Shakita laughed, as I agreed with a nod of the head. "Fuck that, text him. We already know he's mad, but I don't think he'll be as mad once he finds out the truth."

"I don't know. Islande is unpredictable and a lil' crazy. He's coldhearted too, bitch. You see how he left my ass ten years ago."

"You got a point bestie. Just send him a text message."

"I'm not telling that man through a text message. Are you fuckin' crazy? I think you've had one too many shots."

"Bitch, this is only my third one," she said, turning up the shot glass as a bit of liquor ran down her mouth.

"Good for yo' ass," I teased.

"Hush bitch, now, text that man. I ain't saying tell him, but do tell him that y'all need to talk. He'll hit you back."

"Okay."

Islande, I know you may not wanna talk with me, but if you'd let me explain. Can we please talk? NESSA

"Wassup bitch, what you doing?" Shakita asked.

"Just washed Mir and, now, we're about to eat."

"What you cooked?"

"His favorite, mac and cheese and chicken fingers."

"He gon' turn into a chicken finger."

I laughed. "Leave my baby alone."

"So, it's been a whole week. You still ain't heard back from Islande?"

"No girl. I started to just tell him in a text message, but that wouldn't be right. So, if he don't call or text me back, then it must not be something he needs to know."

"Damn, that's crazy though. That nigga is mad, mad. Like mega mad, mucho mad, super mad—"

"Bitch, I get it. Yes, he's pissed the fuck off about me having a baby. I just don't get it though. Even if Mir wasn't his, why be mad? He left me."

"That's right bestie. Men— can't live with 'em. Can't live without 'em."

"I believe I can live without 'em."

"You a whole lie. You like to fuck bitch."

I laughed, "Bitch, you the hoe."

"No ma'am," she busted out laughing. "Don't do me, bitch."

"So, is Islande still in town?"

"From what I'm told. I called Mrs. Pierre just to beat around the bush hoping she'd say something about him, and she did."

"What she said?"

"That he was still in town and that she wished he'd stay this time. However—"

"What bitch?"

"He told her that he'd be leaving to go back next week."

"Wow, are you serious?"

"Yeah, but she said that maybe he's gonna come back though."

"You probably should've just told her."

"Oh, she already believes that Mir is his son, but she can't figure it out. For one, she has never even seen him. It's been three years and that lady has not seen my baby."

"That's wild though."

"Shit, I hardly ever see her myself. But I used to just tell her that mama had him. She didn't make any major efforts to see him but only because I believe she respected my boundaries and I appreciated that."

"Yeah, but that should make them more suspicious."

"The only thing that puzzles her is knowing that I haven't seen Islande. Although she thinks I have but just didn't tell her. You know back when we had his sperm frozen, nobody knew about that in his family. He didn't want them to know. I only told you and Mama, so that was it. But I'm certain he has forgotten all about that."

"Well—you about to jog his memory bestie, in due time."

"Yeah but, if he leaves and I don't get to talk to him, I guess I'll be back at square one because I ain't running his ass down."

"That's unfortunate."

"Sure as hell is, but I've done my part."

"I just think it's been three years too long. Mir deserves to know now—"

"I know, so just hush please. You sound like mama. Hell, she even said if she sees him, she's telling him."

"Ion blame her, but I couldn't cross those lines. I'll just stay in my lane."

"Thanks bitch."

"You're welcome hoe," she teased, as I laughed. "Anyway, do you have some *Baby Luv Lush* or *Dreamsicle Lush*?"

"Girl, you ain't about to be using up all my damn products. You better order some."

"I did last night."

I popped my lips. "Bitch, what's the site then?'

"*The Spiritual Tea Company.* Damn, see, I remembered. Plus, the label is on the fucking products."

I grinned. "Oh, cause I know yo' slick ass."

"I'm in love with that shit. I used all my body wash that you'd given me."

I rolled my eyes. "The only thing I have that I'll probably let you get is my *Unicorn Kisses* and that's only because I just ordered some more."

"Ooooh, I feel special cause that's yo' favorite."

"Well, I have a few favorites now but anyway. You coming to get it because I ain't bringing it to you."

She smacked her lips. "You need to move closer to the city. Old outskirts, hidin' ass bitch you."

I laughed out loud. "Bye bitch!"

"Byeeee," she laughed.

Instant thoughts of Islande crossed my mind. I really wanted to come clean and be honest with him, but he was acting real stank. It had been a week and he'd yet to hit me back. Shit like that bothered me. I really wanted to just let it be, but a part of me was telling me otherwise. However, I had no clue how I could tell him this shit if he wouldn't respond back. Maybe I did need to pay him a visit. Then again— fuck that.

ISLANDE "REMY" PIERRE

I looked over at Santana, as he was texting and driving. He swerved just a bit, as I shook my head. "Nigga, don't kill me before we can get to where the hell we're going."

He laughed. "Man, this girl been on my ass ever since I let her taste my dick."

I grinned. "Damn, lil' Fran is a lil' spicy, ain't she?"

"Hell yeah. I invited her to the room last night and shit, before I knew it, my dick was down her throat."

"Wow, I never pictured her to be so aggressive," I laughed. "But, hey, it be the quiet ones that are freaks."

"You got that right, but Ion know 'bout her being so quiet. She had already showed up kinda tipsy and then when she saw that I was drinking, she wanted more. That liquor had her telling me all her business."

"Like what?"

"She was talking about the restaurant and how she loves working there. Cooking is of course her favorite thing in the world. She also mentioned her son. She said his dad doesn't really claim him or is in his life like that but, hopefully, things will change."

"So, I take it they aren't together."

"Nah, I don't believe the nigga from around here."

"Why you say that?"

"Cause she mentioned something about being tired of having to meet him."

I frowned. "Oh okay. Well, at least you don't have to worry 'bout no baby daddy drama."

"Shit, I wasn't worried either way. Nigga come round me and get his head split."

I grinned. "You got that right."

"Shit, I want Shakita though. The chick that was at the club. She gave me her number, but I just ain't used it yet. I wanted to test the waters a lil' bit first. I got a feeling she gon' give me a run for my money."

"If she's anything like her best friend, I'd say you better tread lightly. They damn sholl don't play."

Santana laughed. "Have you talked to Vanessa yet?"

"Hell nawl. She text and said that we needed to talk, but I don't wanna talk about her having no baby. I mean, I ain't got nothing against the lil' fella, but his mama can go straight to hell."

"Damn nigga. That's harsh. I think you're being a lil' cold towards her. You act like you didn't leave that woman at the altar and shit. Don't do her like that."

I just looked over at him. One thing about Santana, he was gon' keep it all the way 100, whether I liked it or not.

"You know I ain't lyin'. You should talk to her."

"I don't know about that."

"You still in love with her. That's why you acting crazy."

"I don't know if I can get down with her knowing she got a baby daddy somewhere lurking."

"Well, at least it ain't rent-a-cop's," Santana clowned with laughter.

"I don't know if that's good or not. That means she was giving that pussy out to anybody."

Santana frowned. "It definitely don't mean that. Hell, even if she fucked three niggas in ten years, that ain't bad. I know bitches that fuck ten niggas in two months."

I laughed. "Hell, in one week for some."

"Exactly. You shouldn't be so hard on her. You're lucky she ain't married and dodging yo' ass."

"Well, you're right." I shrugged. "But, I don't know. I need some time to process this shit. Hell, I could've had 'bout five kids by now but I didn't want no baby by none of dem broads I was fuckin'. I thought she would've felt the same way."

"Not how you left her."

"Plus, she was having trouble even carrying a child. She never made it past four months I believe. We took extra measures just in case we needed to cross that bridge later in life, but my path led me in a different direction."

"You're regretting that now, huh?"

"A lil' bit," I admitted. "I didn't realize how much I still cared for her until we came face to face. A part of me was hoping she felt that same energy."

"Who says she didn't?"

"Nawl, not after finding out she got a kid. That shit threw me for a loop."

"I see," Santana said. "GPS says that we're almost there."

I looked out the window to see that we had just crossed over into Columbine, Georgia. I glanced in the rearview to see Wesley tailing us.

"You don't think this girl is playing us, do you?"

"She better not be after that five-thousand dollars I gave her po' ass."

"So, you think she's 'bout that life?"

"Hell yeah. Her youngest two kids are by the nigga that died in the hospital. The nigga we're scoopin' up is her baby daddy's brother. She didn't even care for her baby daddy, let alone his brother. She said the nigga ain't never take care of his children. Plus, he used to beat her ass when him and the brother lived with her. She said the brother used to laugh about the shit like it was funny seeing her get beat on."

"Oh well, in that case—she definitely want some get back and we're just the people to help her with it."

"Same thing I was thinking. I told her that once the job was done, she'd get her other ten thousand for helping us. Trust me, she want that money. Shorty don't look like she's had it easy for a long time."

"Damn, how many kids she got?"

"Shit, she told me six and got one on the way by that deadbeat ass nigga."

"Well— he's certainly dead, that's for sure."

Santana laughed, "As a doorknob."

I laughed, "And ironically, we didn't even have nothing to do with that. The police did our dirty work."

"That part." Santana grinned. "So, do you think it was a good thing to bring your mom?"

I glanced back through the rearview at Gaelle's car that Wesley was driving. Joe and Natacha was riding in it with him.

"What you thinking bro?"

"I don't know what I'm thinking." I shrugged. "She insisted on coming, so I let her come."

"How has it been talking to her this past week?"

"I don't know. It hasn't been bad though. We've been catching up here and there, but I'm still not trying to get too attached. I appreciate the conversation or her just calling me, but I don't wanna move too fast. I'm just taking it one day at a time. I prayed on it and well— that's what my heart feels, so that's what I'm going with."

"Well, you have the right to feel how you feel. At least you're talking to her. With your stubborn, coldhearted ass, that's a plus for anybody."

I laughed. "You might be right, nigga."

Santana pulled into the store, as Wesley followed suit. He parked the car, as Santana drove off. Hopefully, this plan would go smoothly. If so, we'd get the answers we'd been waiting for.

"I still can't believe the police don't know shit."

"They move slow as fuck, but you know I don't play about shit like this. I'm on it."

"I already knew I had the best man for the job. I'm glad you came through for me, especially after having a loss yourself."

"Yeah, I know, but you know I got your back always."

"I know." I nodded with a sincere smile. After riding for about ten minutes, we pulled up in the back of a rundown house. "Damn, she live here?"

"This the address she gave me. She said she was going to invite him over, so for us to just come through the back and catch him off guard."

"Man, I don't know. This shit seems like a setup."

"Now that you mention it, you might be right. But if she play me, she gon' wish like hell she didn't."

"So, we just go in?"

"Yeah, we're right on time," he said, looking at the time on the dashboard. "I told her no phone calls or texts. I'm very discreet. Nothing can get traced back to me because that leads to you, and we ain't having that shit."

"That's why I fucks with you the long way." I nodded. "So, let's go."

We got out the car and walked up to the backdoor just like Santana was told. At that time, the door quickly opened, as I grabbed for my piece. But it was just the girl. She was actually quite cute, nice frame, plain Jane but, awkwardly, something I saw lots of potential in.

"Come in. He fell asleep," she whispered.

"Oh good. He's making it easy," Santana joked. "You good?"

"Yeah, but I'm scared. If he wakes up and knows I'm behind this, I'm good as dead."

"Nawl, he's good as dead. Don't worry," Santana said.

"Well, please— y'all hurry up. My kids are on the way back with my sister."

"No problem," Santana said.

She stopped and pointed down the hall but made a U-turn and went the other way. I didn't know what the hell was going on, but I was ready for whatever. The hall took us directly into a living room where the tv was playing Wheel Of Fortune. The screen was pretty staticky and hard to see, but I definitely heard the wheel spinning and the players calling out letters.

The area was lit up from the curtains pulled back as the sun shined through 'em. It was probably the highlight of their day, I was sure. However, it really gave me a glimpse into the world she and her kids lived in. It was indeed roach infested. Them lil' critters was crawling all over the place like it belonged to them. From the looks of things, it did. The sofa was ripped up and dingy as hell with holes in it. I didn't see how they even sat on it. Dirty toys were lined against the wall like she had called herself cleaning up before we arrived. The walls were nasty but not from fingerprints or kid play, but just old and dirty looking. It did smell like Pine Sol, which helped just a little. Like I said, she looked like she had potential. She just needed the right plan to make her dreams come true, and I was just the man for that.

Santana patted me and pointed. Sure enough, dude was knocked out in a shabby looking recliner chair, slobbin' out his mouth and snoring like a drunken sailor. Homeboy was 'bout to have a bad day. I walked over and stood in front of him. I needed the pussy to know it was me that had caught him slipping. I tapped his ass to wake him up and, as he opened his eyes, I smiled at him. It took him a second to realize that a nigga was in his face but, when he did, he tried to jump up. I punched that nigga so hard, I put his ass back to sleep. Santana looked over at me.

"Damn, that fuckin' one hitter quitter ain't no joke."

I arrogantly chuckled. "Too bad they don't be knowing that. Now, let's tie this nigga up and toss his ass in the trunk."

We ended up in a deep section of the city outskirts, somewhere in the fuckin' boondocks in the middle of nowhere.

"Look, homegirl definitely want this nigga gone. You see how she smiled when I was carrying his ass out the house?"

"Hell yeah, but you seen that house? I told you she need that money bad as hell."

"Oh, yeah. She definitely need that. I'm gon' even throw in some extra just for her cooperation."

"I knew you would. Anyway, you think he gon' talk?"

"I hope he do."

"Well, the chick said that the baby daddy mentioned that they'd handled some business that was getting them paid. Apparently, he got the money but didn't give her none, and that's what made it so easy for her to talk."

"So, somebody definitely paid for the hit."

"Definitely seems like it but we're about to find out."

We sat parked for about ten minutes, then Wesley pulled up. We'd left our cell phones, so they'd register back home just in case they found this nigga's body and wanted to connect it to somebody. Matter of fact, Royal had mine pretending to be me as she was told to message Regan and Lisa. Regan probably wasn't going to text back, but I knew Lisa would. I just wanted some play to be coming from my cell phone just in case. Santana had his lil' burner phone, but that was so we'd have some kind of communication if we needed it. But we had no concern about that phone. Plus, I saw him power it off after he'd sent that text. The only thing we banked on was time and, with time, we had all of our moves mapped out.

We got out the car, as I walked around to the trunk.

"That nigga in there?" Wesley asked.

"Hell yeah," I responded and looked over at Santana "You can open it."

Santana popped the trunk, as the nigga's eyes stretched bigger than a Kennedy fifty cent. He was mumbling through the duct tape, veins poppin' out the side of his neck. I bitched slapped his ass. "Shut up nigga. Ain't nobody asked you nothing yet."

In no time, we had that nigga tied up to a tree, really out in the middle of nowhere. I didn't know how homegirl knew about this area but, being as hood as she was, no fuckin' tellin'. I ripped the duct tape off his mouth.

"Remember me, nigga?" I calmly asked.

"No! Who the fuck are you?!" he barked like he was that guy or something.

"The nigga yo' brother tried to kill about a week ago at the club."

"Nigga, I ain't never seen you before! I ain't got nothing to do with what Corey tried to do to you. He dead now, my nigga. That ain't my debt to pay."

"Oh, but do you remember me?" Wesley asked as he walked up on the nigga. It was almost like the nigga had seen a ghost. "You do remember seeing me, huh?"

"Nigga, I ain't have nothing to do with that."

Wesley punched that nigga so hard in his face, blood and teeth spat out his mouth.

"Hold up cuz. Hold up," I intervened, already knowing we was gon' beat this nigga's ass like nobody's business, but we needed answers first.

"Did you fuckin' kill my people?!"

"I—I—"

"Talk nigga before I fuck yo' ass up!" I growled, as Joe just came out of nowhere and punched him so hard in the stomach, the nigga started throwing up.

"Y'all chill for minute," I told 'em. "We need answers. We can't kill him." I waited til the nigga caught his breath and got his shit together. "You see these niggas ain't playin' with yo' ass. You better start talking, and I mean quick or you gon' be left out here to die."

"Y'all niggas gon' kill me anyway," the nigga cried out.

"Nawl, I don't plan on it as long as you start talking. I mean, you could leave here and get some new teeth, heal yourself by any means necessary, but you can't get another life."

He stood helpless with much to think about but in so little time to make his plea. Like a jaybird, that nigga started singing like his life depended on it. "Corey was hired to do a hit that would pay him fifty-thousand-dollars. He asked for my help, and he'd give me ten thousand. All I had to do was drive. So, I joined him. I didn't know who the hell it was that he'd been told to take out," he explained in between crying and trying to catch his breath. "All I knew was that it was a girl and two men involved, and that's after we watched y'all the whole day."

"So, y'all was watching us nigga?!" Wesley asked while walking up on him, as I tugged his shirt to stop him in his tracks.

"Yeah," he admitted. "Please don't hit me. I can't take no more."

I stepped in front of Wesley because this time, he was probably gon' kill him if he hit him again.

"Who was behind the hit? That's all we wanna know. Who sent y'all muthafuckas?!"

The boy wept like a herd of babbling sheep. "Ole hot head ass nigga name Tony was in on it, too. I only met him twice, but I could tell he was a real killer by the shit he said. He was the one that recruited my brother. He was with us in the passenger seat next to me when the shit went down."

I frowned. "Tony Cannon?"

"Yeah, I think that's what my brother said. He was the one that got out the car and shot the nigga who was shootin' back at us."

My heart dropped to my knees. I knew that nigga had something to do with this. I just knew it.

"Damn," I heard Santana say.

I reached my fist back to sock this nigga again, but he screamed out like a lil' bitch. "It wasn't him that put the hit on them though!"

I frowned with a confused look. "What nigga?!"

"It wasn't Tony behind the hit. I think he just wanted to be a part of it. Kept saying something about how some nigga killed his brother years ago and he wanted get back."

"Okay, so who the fuck was behind the hit?!" I roared, now just losing my patience.

"It was a woman. I don't know her name, but she paid my brother the money. She wanted that lady out the way. That's all I know," he cried out. "She wanted that lady gone. That's what Tony kept saying."

"So, a woman wanted Lovely out the picture?" Joe asked with a puzzled expression.

"Yeah."

"A woman was behind the hit?" Wesley asked again to be sure. He was just as confused as the rest of us.

"Yeah, a lady. I didn't see her, but my brother had met her to get the money. She paid him cash inside a brown paperback. He didn't tell us much else, but I knew the hit came from her."

I couldn't take no more. I rocked that nigga's tater so hard, the tree shook, but Natacha swerved around me so quick, I didn't even see her coming. As my heart raced and my ears popped from the explosive sound, she had let off three rounds right in the nigga's face.

"Oh daaaamnn!" Santana let out. "It's time to go."

As I entered the hotel suite, I plopped down in the office chair right behind the desk and dropped my head down, resting on my arms. The evening had been one for the books and I was drained, not only from what I'd learned but also from what I'd witnessed.

"Damn, yo' mama is coldblooded. I see where y'all get that shit from," Santana said.

I just shook my head. "I wasn't expecting her to do that. I mean, I know what she did last week, but she's getting quite good at this shit."

"Yo, they fucked with the wrong family. I know that."

"Definitely did," I agreed. "Wesley said they made one pit stop on the way back and that was for her to throw it over the bridge. She didn't even speak then. Wesley said she tapped him on the shoulder and nodded towards the bridge. He comprehended just what she wanted. The rest of the ride from her was in silence."

"Man, you gotta wonder what she's really going through or thinking about. She had just come face to face with the nigga that shot her daughter, my sister. Yeah, his brother and Tony bitch ass was involved but damn!" I let out. "That definitely had to be a lot for her because it was a lot for me."

"I know man, I know."

"Tony will get his. We can't make no sudden moves because they're already watching us, but he is definitely gonna pay for this."

"Revenge is a dish best served cold."

"Exactly." I nodded.

"Now, about this woman. Who could want Lovely out the way?"

"Especially to a point where they had to kill her," I added.

"Well, let me think on this. It's gotta be somebody that knows she was pregnant."

I frowned. "Why you say that?"

"Because why else would you want her gone? It couldn't have been nothing she did or she would've been gone if it was that bad."

"True."

"So, did Rod have another baby mama or girlfriend—" he paused while thinking. "Maybe even a wife that Lovely didn't know about?"

"I don't know but you're always on to something."

"I'm telling you, this shit is deeper than a muthafucka. After listening to that nigga confess, I realized that we was really just getting started on this case."

"I know, right."

"Listen, I've been doing this shit since I was fourteen, following my dad 'round the house and helping him with some of his cases. I've seen it all. Ain't nothing I don't know about when it comes to this shit, and I put my last dollar on it being a bitch that's either pregnant by that nigga or has a baby already."

"But who the fuck could that be?"

"I don't know but, somehow, I'm gonna find out. You'll see. Give me a couple of days, if that."

"Whoever she is, her child gon' be without a mama when I'm done with her grimy ass. I can promise you that," I said and meant every word of it. Whoever she was, she had better been somewhere countin' her days because that bitch had to go and that was on every thang.

"Well, I got company coming over. So, we'll catch up tomorrow."

"Who coming?" I nosily asked.

"You already know. I enjoyed that wet mouth last night." He grinned.

"Damn, wish I was gettin' some of that."

"Call Nessa."

"Nawl, I'll just jack," I clowned. A part of me really wanted to call Nessa, but my stubborn demeanor always had a way of getting the best of me. I guess that call wouldn't happen no time soon, but if she showed up here again, I might just give in.

FRANCINE "FRAN" BARNES

I sat in the car for a minute trying to gather my composure. I didn't know how to act being that this nigga had called me over again. There really was no one I was that attracted to but him. He was that guy. Hell, it seemed like my feelings for him had grown so quickly, even I couldn't believe it. All I wanted was the nice brick house with the white picket fence and maybe, just maybe, he was the one that could make my dreams come true.

I got out the car and, in no time, I found myself knocking on the door. Butterflies swarmed my stomach. It was something about his handsome face that did something to me. His voice, his walk, his whole existence was a vibe. I was feeling him way more than I should've been, but I couldn't help it. We had a bond, and nothing or no one could ever change that, no matter what.

The door swung open, as I was greeted with a casual smile. "Come in," he said, as I followed him inside.

"I'm glad you called," I said.

"I just think it's time for us to talk, especially with all the shit that has been going on."

I just stood in his foyer area, staring at him. I couldn't read his exterior but, for me to be here, it was definitely a plus. "How are you?"

"I'm well, I guess," he responded.

"I mean, I'm asking because of everything that has been going on."

"I'm good," he repeated, now walking further in as I followed behind him.

For me, I guess now was just as good a time to just be blunt with what I really wanted to say. I mean, if we were going to talk, then let's really talk. "I know you and Lovely were a couple and everything"

Rod just stared at me at first. "How did you know about me and Lovely?"

"Well—uh—you know I work with Royal. Of course, my best friend was going to tell me all about y'all's love affair after that foul shit that happened to them. I just didn't say nothing to you. I really just wanted to keep the peace. I know every time we talk it's an argument and I didn't want that, so I kept quiet."

"Yeah, well, that ain't why I called you over here, but since you wanna make it known then so be it—"

"No—no, you're right. Um—what did you want me to come over for? I figured you wanted to spend time with the baby."

He shook his head and pointed over to the sectional for me to sit down. "No, not yet, but we'll get to that."

"Mm-kay," I uttered while sitting. "So, wassup?" I pondered, wanting this nigga to just speak his mind, so I could know what I was really here for.

"Well— I don't know if you know this, since Royal has been telling you stuff, but Lovely was pregnant with my baby."

"Wow, so you had another baby on the way?" I asked, like I didn't already know.

"Yeah, but they're both gone now," he sadly said, trying to keep his composure.

"Wow," I let out again. "I figured something deep was going on after the last time we talked. I mean, you practically told me to stay out yo' life and that you'd take care of our son from afar. Not that you've ever wanted it to be known anyway. I've had to lie about who he really belongs to just to protect yo' name or shall I say your relationship. One that you never cared to fully share with me," I slid in, trying not to look mad about it. "Hell, y'all hid that shit from everybody."

"Yeah, but I was planning on coming clean about my son, one day. You just never own up to yo' bullshit. I mean, you're a lil' crazy, unpredictable and I had to figure out how to navigate around that."

"What you mean crazy? I've only been trying to prove my love since my son came into this world. He deserves a daddy."

"Yeah, you're right. But I was already in a relationship—"

"With a woman that nobody knew about."

"Whatever, we had our reasons. Having a baby by you was something that I had to figure out. It wasn't like we were in the best of space anyway. You got pregnant on purpose. I know you did. You told me yourself you had stopped taking your pills."

"I said I forgot to take 'em one day. I didn't think that one day would make a difference."

"I really don't believe that but okay, if you say so."

"And that's why we're always arguing. You never believe me."

"You don't really have a good track record of being honest. You tend to bend the truth."

"That's a lie."

"Okay, like the time you ran out of gas right in front of my house. I don't know how long you'd been sitting out there, but you claim you were going to drop off some food to one of my neighbors, but there was no food in your car. I peeped that but I didn't say nothing. I just made sure you got what you needed."

"The food was in the trunk."

"Look, and this is why we argue."

"Okay, leave it alone. I know what happened," I huffed.

"If you say so," he irritably mumbled.

Okay, maybe the food wasn't in the trunk, but I just wanted to check on him. However, he would've taken that as stalking him, so I had to make up something when my shit ran out of gas on my ass. I didn't see how I didn't catch that light blinking over and over again. Guess I was just on a mission that day. Ironically, it was only after I'd just seen Lovely leaving his house. After that, I'd ride through incognito; then, I got caught.

"We could've been a couple from the start had you let that go."

"Why? I loved her. Hell, I'll always love her. And whether you believe it or not, our relationship status was about to change. She was starting to feel like *fuck the world*, it was going to be *us* regardless."

"Well, it took her long enough," I said, trying not to spazz out. "But, if you were a man, like the man that she really needed, you would've been honest about our situation. If she loved you like that, she would've stayed regardless," I mocked. "Not only were you hiding the fact that we'd fuck around—"

"Two times, let's be clear. It was only two fuckin' times and that was only because I wanted to come out to the public about my love for Lovely, but she still was very hesitant and felt we should wait."

"Which is why you shouldn't have been with a woman like that in the first place."

"Nevertheless," he said, overtalking me. "I did some foul shit by fuckin' around with you. I don't know if it was get back for her walking out on me that morning or just me being in my feelings— probably both. But you were there with your comfort food and listening ear." He frowned just out the blue. "How long did you say you knew about Lovely because I'd been confiding to you for a while now?"

"Um—I um— didn't know until after they were killed. I told you Royal told me."

"You sure?"

"Yeah, I already said that, so why you asking me again?" I questioned, feeling a lil' cornered.

"I just asked," he responded in a calmer tone. "You used to stalk me though. I'd wake up to you peeping in my windows and shit—"

"Yeah, but you know that was just me wanting to make sure you were good. You seemed very distraught at one point over her. Well— I don't mean her exactly because I didn't know who it was at the time. But, she had done a number on you."

"Okay, I hear you. I might've been going through some things, but I didn't think it was that deep for you to be peekin' in my windows and shit."

"That was only because I'd rang the doorbell—"

"That I didn't hear."

"Yeah, well—like I said. I'd rang the doorbell a couple of times. I don't know why you didn't hear it."

"Me either," he mumbled with a shake of the head. "I even rang it a couple of times after you left, and it was loud and clear."

"Yeah, whatever—" I slightly sassed. "So, back to why I'm here. I know you didn't call me over just to mention that you and that bi—"

His eyes stretched wide the fuck open and so did my mouth. I couldn't believe I had said that. I could clearly tell that he wasn't too pleased. Matter of fact, he was pissed. I could see it in his face.

"Are you fuckin' kiddin' me right now?! I know damn well you didn't just call this woman a bitch! A woman that was killed in the most horrible way one could imagine while being pregnant with her first child, and this is what you call her?! You got some fuckin' nerves bitch!"

"Hold up, nigga! You don't call me a bitch. I'm the mother of your child!"

"At this point, fuck you and that child! You dirty bitch!"

I swung at him, as he caught my arm. "Turn me loose! You ain't stun my child?! Nigga, I'll air out all yo' dirty laundry."

"Like it fuckin' matters now. But I have to wonder now."

"Wonder what?" I frowned.

"This hatred for Lovely is something I didn't know you had."

"Okay and?!"

"Just get out my house! Get the fuck out! I didn't mean what I said about the baby because he is innocent in all this but I'm watching you, bitch!"

"Fuck you, nigga!" I snapped as I walked out. I was pissed the fuck off but, the minute I got in the car, I felt like I had really fucked up this time. My anger had gotten the best of me to a point that I really might've just blown my own cover. The last thing I needed was anything coming back on me. It definitely wasn't supposed to go down like this. Quickly, I pulled out my cell phone to make an impromptu call. On the first ring, Tony answered.

"Why you calling me?"

"I—we need to talk."

"Not on this line," he said and ended the call.

"Damn," I whispered with a shake of the head. I knew the number one rule was not making these types of calls from our regular cell phones. We didn't need nothing to tie back to us, yet I was unraveling like a muthafucka. I needed a woosah moment or I really was going to fall apart. I definitely had done the unthinkable by putting in motion something that I could never take back, all because I was so deep in my feelings and head over heels in love with a nigga that clearly still didn't want me. Maybe, over time, he'd come to his senses but, right now, I highly doubted it. I really had said a lil' too much and that nigga in there wasn't slow by a long shot. "Aaaaah!" I groaned out loud while hitting my steering wheel. I started my engine and backed out of Rod's driveway in route to somewhere I could clear my thoughts.

"Hey Mama's baby," I said, kissing all over my little one. Anything I did, I did for him. It may not have seemed like it because I worked most times, and he only saw me when I was off. Most times, he'd be staying with my first cousin Ralph and Royal. They treated him like he was their own. I couldn't have been more appreciative of that. But, he was created out of love and, because of that, I loved him with my whole being. Whether Rod stepped up or not, that love would never change.

"What's going on with you?" Ralph asked as he handed me a mixed drink of tequila and peach Red Bull.

"I just have a lot on my mind."

"Apparently, I mean it ain't even noon and you're already drinking. Mind you, a strong drink at that."

"I just have to declutter my thoughts. I feel like I'm all over the place."

"You alright?" he asked, taking Lil' D out of my hands. "He's getting sleepy."

"I know," I said, noticing that he'd started fussing a little.

"Well, hold that thought. I'll be right back."

"Okay," I responded as I started sipping on my drink. My heart was bitter and very torn. Never in a million years did I think I'd ever stoop so low as to be a part of something that I knew was wrong. I brought the shit into existence, but I didn't think it would go as far as it did. I had the power to stop it but, when I tried, it was too late. By then, Tony had all the power and he took over. As I turned my drink up, Ralph joined me. "You laid him down?"

"Yeah, he went straight to sleep too."

"If anything ever happened to me, take care of him for me."

He frowned. "What you mean by that?"

"I'm just saying. You know how life is. It's rather unpredictable and I just wanna make sure my baby will always be in good hands."

"Now, you know me and Royal got you."

"I know, but—" I paused, thinking that I didn't know how Royal would feel if she ever found out what really happened. God only knew, and I was really praying that she never would.

"But what—" he pondered, just as my cell chirped.

I glanced down at the text from an unknown number. The only thing it said was: *get here.*

"But nothing." I smiled. "I know y'all got me. Anywaysss, I need to be going."

"Already?" He frowned.

"Yeah."

"You sure you're good?"

"Yeah, I'm fine," I told him, grabbing my purse to leave. "Kiss my baby for me. I'll call you later." Before he could keep grilling me, I quickly left.

———◦⬥◦———

As I sat in my car parked at a lowkey location where we used to meet up to get this plan in motion, I spotted Tony pulling up. I was nervous as shit to tell him what kind of morning I'd just had with his brother, but I think it was things that needed to be said.

He jumped in my Range Rover, looking at me like I wasn't the only one with shit on my mind. "Wassup Fran?"

"Shit, wassup with you? The way you're looking got my stomach turning."

"I don't know what's going on, but Corey was killed by the police."

"Yeah, I know. What made him try some dumb shit like that anyway?"

"I don't know what he was thinking. Probably on that fuckin' liquor. I told his ass not to come back this anyway. But he was fuckin' some lil' shawty from around the way."

"Damn, that's fucked up."

"So, he wanted to take out Remy. I did mention that I was putting a thirty-thousand bounty on his head, but that's because I didn't think a nigga could get that close to him. So, of course, that wouldn't have ever happened."

"Well, technically, you were right. He got close but not close enough," I said with a shake of the head. "I'm kinda scared though. I kinda spazzed out at yo' brother's crib today and I really pissed him out. On top of that, he may be thinking something."

"Like what?"

"Like, you know what?"

"He ain't that smart. He'll never put the shit together."

"I didn't mean for shit to go this far. I asked you not to go through with it."

"Yeah, the day of. Hell, I already had them niggas in place. So, I started calling shots. I wasn't about to let James' bitch ass get away this time. I owed him that shit."

"Damn, you were so cold with it. If his family ever finds out, that's our ass."

"Nobody is going to find out. Just chill."

"So, why were you looking crazy when you got in here?"

"For one, don't ever call my fuckin' phone no more like that."

"My bad, I'm sorry."

"Don't be sorry, be careful," he shot back.

"Okay, and what was the other reason?"

"Word on the Columbine streets is that Boogie is missing."

I frowned. "Talking about Corey's brother?"

"Yep," he responded.

"Damn, if Corey got killed by the police and now his brother is missing—hell, I could've kept my damn money."

"The way them boys lived, that money probably was gone in a matter of days anyway. Hell, Corey had about thirteen children by about ten different baby mamas. I'm just glad that neither of them are here to talk. So, that might not be a bad thing. All I know is that from this point on, you need to lay low. If you're not working at the restaurant, chill the hell out. Take care of nephew and stay away from my brother until he calms down."

"Say less."

Once he stepped out of my vehicle, all I could do was think that with the brothers out the way, maybe we were off the hook. Because this could not come back on me or I was going to lose everything, not just Rod but my son, too.

ISLANDE "REMY" PIERRE

As the day before replayed in my mind, all I could think about was Natacha and how ruthless she was. For someone to be as beautiful as she was and once the sweetest woman I knew, she had grown to be a cold-blooded killer and very calculated at that. She didn't give any of us time to knock that nigga off because she wasted no time doing it for us. This must've felt like justice to her, but it also showed me how much she still loved us. The look in her eyes were of sadness mixed with anger. I could only imagine what she would've did to the nigga's brother had the police not intervened and did the job for us. But, then, that left ole pussy ass Tony. I knew that bitch nigga was in on this. Something in my gut told me he did, but was it a planned out hit that also included Rod? That was where my confusion set in. All I knew was that whoever else was involved, they asses had to go too.

A knock sounded off at the door, as I walked over to answer it. Peeping through the peephole, I saw Wesley and Joe standing there. I quickly opened it and let 'em in.

"Wassup Cuz?" Wesley spoke as we hugged, then gave each other dap.

"Shit, tryna see wassup myself."

"Where is Santana?" Joe asked.

"He's on the way," I responded, as they sat down on the sofa and I sat back behind the desk.

"That shit was wild yesterday. I never imagined I'd ever see Auntie doing no gangster shit like that," Wesley said.

"Who would've known that a savage was underneath the broken layers of her whole existence?" Joe chimed in.

"Right." I nodded with a serious face. "And they wonder where we got it from. Hell, that wild shit would've been in us whether we lost our parents or not."

"Same thing I was thinking," Joe said.

"Man, that just tells me that Natacha ain't playing about her offspring or her nephew. I believe she'd rather take matters in her own hands than to let the justice system play those cards. At least with her running shit, she knows the outcome," Wesley acknowledged.

"Mannnnn, that's exactly how I feel about it. He ain't the first one she knocked off."

Joe's eyes stretched. "What you talkin' 'bout?"

"She killed that first nigga too. That ummm— Stoney Harris dude."

"Noooo," Wesley let out.

"Shit, she told me herself."

"Wow," Joe uttered.

"So, she must've thought he had something to do with it?"

I simply nodded my head. "Yep."

"Damn, auntie a real fuckin' beast out here in these streets," Wesley said. "But, aye, I love that shit. Don't fuck with the Pierres or the Baptistes. Yo' ass will get dealt with."

"You ain't neva lied," Joe agreed. "But, yo, who the fuck is the female that's in on this shit?"

I shrugged. "I don't know, but Santana is on it early this morning. Trust me, I bet we know something in a couple of days, if not sooner. He don't bullshit when he gets on a case."

"I see. He had that shit all planned out yesterday with that nigga's baby mama," Joe said.

"Yeah, right down to us scooping that pussy ass nigga up out her living room slobbing—"

"Slobbing?" Wesley grinned.

"Yeah, the nigga was knocked out. I bet he think he's having a wild ass nightmare."

"Yeah, in hell," Joe added.

"Sick as muthafucka. I don't care if he didn't pull the trigger, he still drove for them pussy ass niggas. And Tony Cannon—"

Joe intervened, "Bitch ass nigga gon' get his. I can still picture him standing over my brother and killing him. He walked back to that car like he'd gotten his due vengeance, but he ain't seen shit yet. It took everything in me not to find his ass last night and fuck him up. Luckily, Iesha talked some sense into me."

"Yeah, we can't make no moves right now. They will definitely know it's us. For now, it seems like they're loose ends are kind of tied up because two of the culprits are dead. However, that leaves two more. I believe we have time in finding out who's behind this before the police does and when we do—"

"They better count their days," Wesley acknowledged. "It's gon' be some smoke in the city."

At that time, another knock was at the door. "That's probably Santana. Let him in."

Wesley walked over to the door and in walked Santana with a look of disbelief on his face. His vibe was all thrown off. I'd hung around this nigga for ten years and I'd never seen him glare over at me like he did. Quickly, I asked, "You good nigga?"

"Not really, but I may as well tell y'all what I just found out."

"What?" Joe asked.

"Let me sit down," he said but, right after sitting down, he stood back up. "Ain't no easy way of saying this-"

"So, just say it," I blurted out.

"Well, I had a lil' company last night— let me start there," he said. "It was Fran—"

"Damn, you hittin' that?" Wesley pondered.

"I did last night," he answered. "But, that ain't what I wanna talk about. This morning, she left and said she had to open the restaurant. Of course, after she left, I slid out of bed and decided I'd go grab me some breakfast from the Breakfast Bar. Well, when I pulled up, I saw her car pulling out of the parking lot from behind the restaurant. I don't know, instinct told me to follow her."

My stomach turned in knots. I didn't know where he was going with this, but a part of me kind of did. However, I didn't know how to tie it all together. Like, the shit still wasn't adding up to what I needed to know.

"Where she went?" Joe pondered.

"I followed her to nice suburban area called Sterling Estates."

I frowned. I knew where that was, and I knew who lived there. I looked over at Joe and Wesley. I could tell they also knew or had a feeling where this was probably heading.

"She pulled up to a two-story brick house and sat in the vehicle for a minute or two. I had drove around the block and parked in front of a neighbor's house about two houses down from her but across the street. I could tell she was lost in thought because she didn't even see me. It looked like she was talking to herself. I don't know. She pulled down the visor a few times to check herself and, then, finally, she got out."

"Wow," was all I could muster up to say. I was already shocked.

"She went to the door and a nigga let her in."

"I just know better," Wesley uttered.

"Well, I sat there for almost twenty minutes, if that long. She really didn't stay in there too long before coming back out, pissed off."

"What you mean pissed off?"

"She was mad as hell. Hit the steering wheel when she got in and even screamed out. I could hear her from my car."

"Damn, I wonder what that was about?" Joe pondered.

"So, do y'all think it was Rod's house she went to?" Wesley asked.

"That's the only nigga I know that stays over there," I said, having already found out the whole family's location the first day I touched down. "Something is off. Fran has been in the family for a long ass time. She and Royal are like best friends. Hell, Royal has been dating Fran's cousin since they were in middle school. I just don't see her doing this. Do you think she could've been questioning him or something? Maybe she's looking for answers too."

"I thought about that," Santana said. "But—"

"You think it's something more?" I pondered.

"I'm thinking maybe she was fuckin' the nigga."

Our eyes stretched. "You ain't heard nothing about them, Wes?"

"Nawl, nothing. I mean, Fran is pretty private. I don't even believe I ever seen her baby daddy. He don't even live around here."

"Orrr—" Santana dragged with lines of confusion written across his forehead. "This nigga Rod could be the baby's daddy."

"Oh wow," Wesley let out. "Don't tell me that could be true."

"If it is, then she was the female that wanted Lovely out the way. It makes sense," Joe responded with an almost skeptical shake of the head.

"This can't be," I uttered. "This can't be."

"It's pointing in that direction," Joe said.

"What's her baby's name?" I pondered.

"They call him lil' D," Wesley responded. "It's only one way to find out. Call your sister."

I frowned. "I don't know about that. Calling her might not be in our best interest right now. We need to really find out if she's behind this first. Another thing, we can't tell my mama. That girl probably be found dead inside the restaurant—" I said as a lightbulb went off in my head. "Speaking of the fuckin' restaurant— that sign in the front is blue with blinged out sparkles around it. The name of the restaurant is Fran's Breakfast Bar."

"Wow," Wesley let out. "This shit is getting even crazier, the more we talk about it. I just can't believe that lil' cute Fran could be this deceiving."

"Shit, I just fucked her last night. I didn't pick up on that energy."

"Probably because yo' dick was down her throat the minute she entered yo' room."

Santana grinned a little. "You could be right Joe."

"Damn, this shit got my head spinning," I said, lying my head down on the desk.

"I know, right. I just can't believe it. Fran cooks for the family a lot. Royal and Ralph is always keeping the baby. She was pretty close with Lovely and James too. Like, she has truly been a family friend. She just cooked for us the day we buried them. Like, what the fuck?! With friends like her, who the hell needs enemies?!"

"You right," Joe agreed with a shake of the head.

"I can't believe it's led to this. When should we tell Royal? I really believe she should know. She could probably put the missing pieces together for us."

I shrugged. "I'm sure, but this shit is so fuckin' sensitive. Fran is the head cook at the restaurant. I don't really know if she co-owns the place or not, but there is also a baby involved that could be Rod's that has a huge presence in Royal's life. There is also the history of their friendship-"

"That bitch ain't no friend," Wesley cut in. "I really wanna go to that restaurant and hold that bitch head down in a pot of hot boiling grits. Maybe even a pot of collard greens— dirty bitch. Drown that slut bucket," he added with anger in his eyes. "I should put Gaelle on her trick ass—"

"Cuz, calm down," I eased in. I knew he was pissed the fuck off. Hell, we all were. "We can't let our emotions get the best of us. It's a lot at stake."

"Nothing's at stake but that bitch head when I'm finished with her."

"Wes, chill yo," I said again. "She's gettin' what's coming to her. That's a fact. It's just all in due timing."

"You can't say nothing, Wes. We don't wanna tip off Tony, who is the nigga I really wanna smoke. I owe that bitch nigga some hot lead up the ass."

"You and me both. But, we can't move like that. Nobody in here wants to go to prison for murder. We got too much to live for. Unfortunately, Lovely and James was robbed of that, but we'll get vengeance for them. That's coming, without a doubt."

"I just need some fresh air. I'm going home to clear my head."

"You can't say nothing, not even to Gaelle," I reminded him. "Please, cool off but don't say a word about this."

"I think we need to say something sooner than later."

"I agree Wes. Maybe even as early as in the morning, but I'm still on the fence right now."

"A'ight," he said, walking to the door. "Y'all hold it down. I'll call one of y'all later. I need a fuckin' drink."

"Wesley!" I called out. "Don't say nothing."

"I'm not, nigga," he said while dropping his head and walking out to leave. He closed the door behind me, as I looked over at Joe. "You think he gon' say something?"

Joe shrugged. "It's hard to say but I hope not."

"I know right," Santana said as his cell phone began to ring. He looked down at the display of his screen. "Damn, it's her—"

"Who, Fran?" Joe asked.

"Yeah."

"You answering it?"

"Shit, I don't want to," Santana said. "This shit is crazy as fuck. I've never been involved with someone that I was potentially investigating."

"Answer it, so she don't be thinking nothing," I told him.

"Nah, I don't know 'bout that. I'll just text her later," he responded. "I wouldn't even know what to say to her."

"Ion blame you," Joe uttered. "I might call that bitch out if I hear her voice."

"Well, in that case don't answer," I quickly said. I really had to think about this shit. I didn't know what to do at this point, but something definitely needed to be done.

"I feel like Wesley. I just need some air. I'm going to my room for a bit. Call me later," Joe said as he gave me and Santana dap. He wasted no time getting leaving either.

I looked over at Santana. "I guess you leaving too?"

"Hell yeah. Shit, I feel like I just fed my dick to a fuckin' snake."

I frowned, just staring at his crazy ass. "Damn, you feel violated now, don't you?"

"Hell yeah, like I just wanna go crawl under the covers and get my mind right."

I wanted to laugh but I couldn't even muster nothing up. "Damn, I feel you. I'll call you later. I'm 'bout to lay down myself."

"A'ight bro," Santana said as he gave me dap and then, just that fast, I was left alone with nothing but a bottle of Armand de Brignac Ace of Spades Champagne, a bottle of Clase Azul Gold Tequila and my thoughts.

I stepped out of the shower about eight sheets in the wind. I didn't know how I managed to even stand there that long. I'd drank over half the bottle of champagne and more than a few shots of tequila, just trying to cope with the shit that I'd just found out. I mean, we didn't have any solid evidence but, damn, all the shit surrounding Lovely and James' death pointed directly at Fran. She was the woman that wanted my sister out the way. I didn't know how Tony tied into that but somehow he did, and I was so fuckin' hot about it. I had all intentions on paying Rod a visit but, for now, it didn't seem like he had nothing to do with it. However, only time would tell.

As I walked in the bedroom of the suite, I picked up my cell phone to see that I had two missed calls from Lisa and one missed call from Nessa. I hadn't talked to Nessa since the last time she was here. She had been trying to get in touch with me, but I wasn't with it. Now, having had nothing but time to think about the shit, I guess I was wrong in a lot of ways. I couldn't be mad at her for having a child by another nigga. I'd done her wrong and I guess I deserved that shit. I really should've seen it coming. Like, who the fuck did I think I was? I pondered while giving it some thought. Shiiiit, I was the muthafuckin' man. Ain't no way I was psyching myself out that bad. Still, I guess I should've seen that coming.

Shit really just took me by surprise because I'd kept a close eye on her social media accounts over the years, and she never was posted up with a nigga and she damn sholl didn't post pictures of a baby. I would've remembered that shit. If nothing else, Nessa had become a very private person. It had to be a pleasure just being able to see her at her place of business. I knew niggas drooled over that fat ass and pretty face, which was very smart of her to have rent-a-cop's ole pussy ass at the door or on security there. I was sure he watched everybody that watched her. But, I was too smooth for a nigga. Couldn't watch me and ya girl. Yo' ass gon' be lost in the sauce tryna keep up with what I had going on. I promise ya.

My phone rang. I glanced down to see that it was Lisa calling back. I answered, "Wassup Lisa?"

"Damn, since you been in the dirty south, a bitch can't catch up with you."

I grinned. "It ain't like that."

"Oh, yes, the hell it is," she teased with soft laughter. "How are you? I miss you."

"I'm okay," I responded as I laid back on the bed, closing my eyes. "You miss me, huh? Or do you miss this dick?"

She laughed, "Both of y'all big headed asses."

I grinned. "How you been?"

"I'm good. Me and my nigga called it quits."

"Who left who?"

"He left me; can you believe it? How the hell a nigga leave all this?"

"Shit, I can believe it. Ain't no way my lady walking round the damn house with another nigga's name tatted on her titty. I can see if it was old, but that's a new fuckin' tattoo."

"It says *Islande*. That could mean I wanna be on vacation somewhere on a fuckin' Island."

"Woman, if you don't quit," I laughed. "The *Islande* on yo' titty got a *e* behind it."

She laughed. "But it's got the look of paradise in the background."

I chuckled. "You funny yo. I can't blame that damn man. I would've been surprised if he stayed."

"Whatever—so, did it turn you on that I'd gotten tatted?"

I frowned. "Hell nawl. You ain't my woman."

"But I wanna be."

"Nawl, I can't do it like that. I like you and all. Don't get me wrong, but I ain't ready for that."

"You ain't gettin' no younger."

"You ain't neither, so you better go cover up that tatt and get yo' man back."

She smacked her lips. "You know how I feel about you, Islande."

"I know, but I told you to tuck dem fuckin' feelings—"

"Where?" she hissed. "Where exactly am I supposed to tuck 'em?" she asked in a sassy tone.

"Hell, put 'em in ya' pussy or up yo' ass— anywhere but ya' heart. Leave 'em outside before you come in my house— do something with 'em. I can't keep fuckin' with you otherwise."

"Damn, you're a fuckin' cold hearted nigga. You know that?"

I shrugged. "I've been told that a few times before."

"Shiit, I'm sure more than a few—"

"Anyway," I said, cutting her off. I could tell she was getting in her feelings. Something I clearly said she needed to stay out of.

"Well, how long you gon' be gone? I wanted to see you."

"I don't know yet. But, honestly, I think it's best if we just go our separate ways. It's no hard feelings whatsoever. I just got a lot going on right now. I can't be adding no more stress on."

"So, you're saying I stress you?"

"Yeah, because what we had was for fun, and you took that and turned it into something more. I just ain't got time for none of this."

"I'll tuck my feelings—damn! I'll even call Sasha over when you get back, so we can make up for the time you've been away."

I thought about Sasha's fine, freaky ass just from the mention of her name but, for some reason, I felt over that shit. I wanted more. "Nawl, let's just leave this where it's at. Get ya man back. Do something. I can't right now."

"Wow, I can't believe you're breaking—"

"Nawl, not breaking up. We ain't together Lisa."

"You know what I mean."

"Nawl, I don't," I responded, just ready to end this call. "Go on with your life."

"Islande—"

I simply ended the call. Honestly, I was lit. I didn't wanna hear that shit. As I dozed off, I heard knocking. I jumped up. "Who the hell could be coming here?" I knew earlier that everybody else was in their feelings and hauled ass. Maybe Santana had found out something else. Quickly, I made my way to the door but stopped shy of taking another shot of tequila, being that it was on the counter staring at me. "I'm coming!" I yelled out. I was very surprised when I peeped to see who it was.

"Nessa," I said, opening the door. I tried like hell to keep my composure, but she was looking good as hell. The more I stared, the hornier I got. "Damn, I wasn't expecting to see you. What brings you by?"

VANESSA "NESSA" LUCAS

"Well, dang, you gon' let me in or would you rather I leave?" I asked while scoping his fine ass out. Damn, he still had it, and coming to the door in nothing but a white towel wrapped around his waist didn't help. "Move," I said, brushing past him.

He chuckled. "My bad babe. I can't lie, you looking good as fuck."

I looked at him and glanced over on the counter in the kitchen area to see a damn near empty bottle of tequila. "Yo' ass is drunk," I said, directing my attention back at him.

"No, I'm not," he said, walking up on me.

"Islande, chill out," I insisted.

"But what if I don't want to?"

I grinned a little, as he instantly wrapped his arms around me and squeezed my ass. "Back up. We need to talk." I innocently squealed, gently pushing him back.

"Come here. I've missed you," he said, all over me at this point. I knew he was lit. I could smell it on his breath, but I swear it was the best kind of liquor smell ever.

"Islande, stop it. How is it that suddenly you miss me? You haven't responded to my calls or text but, now that I'm back over here, you miss me."

"I do. I ain't lyin'. I was in my feelings, that's all. But I get it. I understand now. You did what you had to do."

"What you mean?" I pondered, pushing him back again. He just wouldn't let up.

"I mean, I get it. You had a baby, but I don't wanna talk about that right now. I just want you."

"Islande, please. We need to talk about that," I said while backing away but, the further I backed up, the closer he got until my back was against the wall.

"This is where I want you."

I frowned. "Where? Here?"

"Yeah, right here," he said while lifting me up, feet off the floor a little. "You wearing the hell out this Fendi skirt," he growled in my ear. "Damn, you smell good."

"Islande, pay attention please," I giggled. I couldn't even be serious with him. He was giving me too much of what I was trying to separate myself from.

"What you think I'm doing?" he teased.

He pressed his body against mine. Damn, this nigga smelled so good. All I wanted to do was show up, so we could talk about Mir and get this shit over with. Yet, he already had other plans that apparently kicked in the minute he saw me. I was scared though. His mood would likely change the minute I confess what I'd done. He was probably gonna be pissed as fuck, either because he didn't want kids by me and I'd done the unthinkable. Or he was going to be pissed that I kept it from him, even though he'd eventually accept it. Either way, he was going to be pissed. I knew him that much, at least.

"Islande, please. I came here to talk."

"Talk about what?" he pondered. "I told you we don't have nothing to talk about. I just wanna feel you. Can I feel you?" he literally begged, as his hand crept up my skirt. I'd dreamed of this moment for over ten years and, now that it was happening, I didn't know how to act or what to feel.

"Listen, can we just talk?"

"No," he said. "Please, just chill out." He stopped once saying that and gazed in my eyes. "You don't want me?"

I gazed back in his eyes. Just staring, wanting to stay on track and talk about what needed to be said but—

"Do you want me, Nessa?"

"Fuuuuck Islande. This ain't what I'm here for."

"Do you want me?"

Fuck it, I thought. "Yes," I passionately responded. "Yes, I want you."

At that moment, I jumped his bones like a fuckin' dog in heat. Like literally, I jumped in his arms as he carried me to the bedroom and laid me on the bed. He wasted no time at all pulling my clothes off and devouring my cookies. Whew, this shit had nothing on his ten years ago self. This nigga was not playing with my ass. He literally had a taste of every part of my body; I mean, from the rooter to the tooter and beyond.

Islande's dick was nothing short of beautiful. It had to be the biggest, prettiest dick I'd ever had. It was thick and solid, kind of like his personality, not to mention he could go great lengths to reach my—

"Islaaaaande!" I called out, as he continued to slither his python deeper inside me.

"I love you," he said, to my surprise. I was so caught off guard, I didn't know what to respond. It was like he didn't even care because he said it again, just in case I didn't hear him. "I love you, Nessa. I love you."

He fucked me so good from the front and then flipped me over on my stomach while entering my slippery slope, causing a gush of ocean tides wetting the sheets.

"That's how you feel?"

"Mh-mm," I moaned. This feeling was like nothing I'd ever experienced, and I was loving every second of it. Next thing I knew, Islande was eating me from the back as my juices quenched his thirst. I drizzled his mouth with passionate showers of black girl magic, unable to contain myself or my emotions. This nigga had me gone— again...

Once I felt like he'd had more than his share of cookies and milk, I turned the tables. I just craved having his cock in my mouth to show him how much I missed it. I toyed with it first while gazing in his eyes. His head fell back as I gently sucked on the head, almost licking it like a lollipop; then, I went in. As spit oozed down my hands, I slurped and sucked almost to a point of throwing up. I wanted it touching my tonsils and crawling down my throat. I wanted his ass bad as hell. I could feel him tensing up, ready to explode, so I quickly slipped it out my mouth and began jacking it so his creamy goods could paint my face.

"Daaaamn," he groaned with a smile.

I walked in the bathroom to clean myself up.

"Where you going?"

"I'll be back."

"No, lay down."

I glanced back at him, almost unable to see with nut everywhere. "Boy, do you see my face? You want me to lay down like this?"

He laughed. "Nawl, gon' clean up."

"I'll bring you a washcloth back."

"Okay," he said, lying back on the bed stark ass naked.

I walked in the bathroom and began washing my face. "Aye, so, about that talk."

"Wassup babe?"

Babe, I thought. It had to be the liquor because this nigga was frisky as hell tonight. "Islande."

"Yeah."

"We still need to talk."

"Okay talk," he said.

"I wanna talk about Mir."

"Who is Mir, babe?"

"My son," I responded. It felt funny to say *our* son when he didn't even know Mir was his yet.

"Babe, we can talk about that later."

"But I need to really talk to you about this now, just in case you decide to put me out afterwards. Hopefully, I can leave with my dignity," I slid in a joke, hoping to lighten the situation. "Just hear me out okay, before you say anything," I paused, waiting for a response but nothing. "Islande!" I called out, now walking back in the room with a warm washcloth. "Islande, hear me out first, okay." This nigga was sleep. "Islande," I said, swoppin' him on the leg.

"Huh?" he said, sitting straight up in the bed.

"You can't fall asleep right now. We gotta talk."

"Come on," he said, pulling me down on the bed with him. "Let's just sleep. We'll talk in the morning."

With that being his last words before dozing back off to sleep, I just laid quietly beside him and, in minutes, I'd fallen asleep too.

I woke up to the sound of Islande's phone ringing off the chain. "Islande," I said, shaking him. "Answer your phone."

He rolled over but doubled back to glance at me. "So, this—we—us, wasn't a dream?"

"No, I'm here in the flesh."

"Thank God." He smiled, leaning over and kissing me. I smiled back, feeling very relieved that he wanted me here with him.

"Please, answer your phone."

He picked it and glanced at the display. "It's just Royal."

"Well, answer it. She must want something. She's called at least twice already."

"Hello," he answered, putting the phone on speaker.

"Remy, I need you to come over to Nana's house right now."

He frowned while staring at me. "Why, you okay?"

"No, please, just get here now!"

"Royal—" he said, but she had already ended the call. "What the fuck?!" he let out while calling her back, but she didn't answer. However, his phone rang again. "It's Wes," he said while answering. "Yo, wassup?"

"Did Royal call you?" he asked.

"Hell yeah," he responded while putting on his clothes.

"Something happened. Me and Gaelle are headed over to Nana's now."

"Damn, me too," he said. "I'll see you when I get there." He ended that call and called Santana. "Get ready.

We're going to Nana's house." He ended that call and called Joe. On the first ring, Joe answered. "Yo, did Royal call you?" he asked.

"Hell yeah. She sounds like she knows something," Joe responded. "She wants us to come over. You ridin' with me?"

"Yeah, me and Santana will be down in a few."

"A'ight," Joe said, as Islande ended that call.

"You good babe?" he asked, now directing his attention at me.

"No, because we still need to talk," I answered but definitely confused by whatever the hell was already going on with him and his family.

"I have a lot going on right now. We can talk when I get back. Unless you wanna ride with me over there, and Joe and Santana can ride together."

"Islande, Mir is your son," I blurted out.

He frowned in the middle of slipping on his shoes. "Come again."

"I said that Mir—"

"Mir who is your son, right?"

"Yes," I answered.

"How is he my son? Nessa, I don't have time for this. I have a family emergency going on right now."

"I'm serious. He's your son."

"How the hell is that baby my son, and I haven't touched or smelled the pussy in over ten years until last night."

"I used your sperm three years ago."

"My sperm?" he questioned, but the look on his face was that of being deep in thought.

"Yeah, remember when we had your sperm frozen just in case we tried to have a baby later. We even entertained the thought of getting a surrogate."

"Wow, you gotta be kidding me right? How was that possible? I didn't give nobody consent—"

"I worked around it."

"So, you mean to tell me that you've had my son for three years, yet nobody knows but you—"

"Me, mama and Kita."

"Nana didn't even know?"

"No, but she had her suspicions. However, I never brought my baby around. I didn't want you to ever hear about this from nobody but me."

"So, as close as you were with my family, you couldn't even confide in Nana?"

"No, because she would've told you and you had left me! Don't forget about that!"

"Oh, I fuckin' remembered," he shot back. "But you been playing it raw for three fuckin' years. You good, I tell ya that."

"I just wanted to protect my son. I didn't know how you'd feel about this."

"So, waiting til now was supposed to make me feel better?"

"No, I'm not saying that, and you have every right to be mad. You don't even have to be in his life. He's fine, he's healthy, he's thriving—"

Islande disappointedly shook his head. "How did you have him? Did they just shoot my sperm up in some random ass lady?"

"No, they put it in me. I had him. He was premature, right at twenty-seven weeks but thank God he survived."

Islande took in a deep breath and let it out. "Wow, and you didn't think I'd wanna know that? Or that I'd even wanna be a part of his life?"

"I promised mama that if you ever came home, I'd confess and tell you."

"So, what if I never came home?"

"Then, you would've never known."

"Wow, this is un-fuckin'-believable. You tell me that I have a child now? A three-year-old son?" he pondered just as his phone rang. Honestly, I was glad because I didn't know what Islande was about to do or say to my ass. "Yeah!" he answered in an angry tone. "Okay, I'm on the way. Calm the fuck down. I'm coming!"

"Is everything okay?" I asked.

"Nessa, I—I—" He took in another deep breath. "This is too much for me right now. We'll talk about it later. I have to go to Nana's."

"You want me to go with you?"

"Um—not right now. I just can't deal with too much and what you just told me is a fuckin' lot."

"Okay, I respect that," I said, now putting on my clothes.

"I gotta go," he angrily expressed and dashed out the room. I just sat in disbelief that I'd actually told him. He was pissed like I knew he would be, but he'd get over it.

He didn't say he didn't wanna be a part of Mir's life, so that was a plus. I just wanted for this to work out between us, mainly co-parent in the same city and state. That long distance shit wasn't something I wanted to do but, either way, I'd have to respect Islande's wishes. I just wished it all worked in me and Mir's favor.

ROYAL "SWEETS" PIERRE

I stood out in the front yard pacing back and forth, definitely in my feelings. The call I'd just gotten was nothing nice and I didn't know how to handle it.

"Babe, come on back inside. It's kinda cold out here," Ralph said.

"I just wanna be left alone for a minute."

"Can you tell me what that call was about then?"

"No, you'll find out when everybody else does," I angrily responded.

I was livid, hurt, and confused. I still couldn't put the pieces together, even though I'd been given more than enough to figure the shit out.

"Well, your mama is pulling up," Ralph pointed. "Oh damn, Wes is behind her," he said, as I looked out beyond the land to see a black Hellcat and a white Range Rover pulling up. "Are you going to do this outside? At least let me get you a coat."

"Please, get me a jacket," I insisted, just so he'd leave me alone. I could barely deal myself and I just needed air to breathe. As he walked in the house, Nana and Josette came outside.

"Royal, it's chilly out here. You sure you don't wanna come inside?"

"No ma'am," I responded. "Y'all come out here. I believe we're all going to need some air by the time I tell y'all this."

"Well, let me get my jacket," Josette said as she headed back in the house. "Get yo' jacket," she told auntie before she could get out on the patio good.

Natacha parked her Range and quickly jumped out. "Royal, what's going on?!"

"Natacha, just chill for a minute. I'm waiting for everybody to get here."

"Is it bad? It's gotta be bad." She said, reading my body language.

"Natacha." I said with a shake of the head.

"Okay," she responded. "Hey Mommy," she then spoke as Nana hugged her.

"Hey baby. I don't know what's going on, but it's something big for Royal to be acting like this."

"I believe I know what it is," Natacha said.

At that time, Wesley and Gaelle got out his car. He rushed over. "What happened?"

"I'll tell y'all when everybody gets here," I said, just pacing back and forth now as everybody spoke to each other while conversing amongst each other with puzzled reactions. I could hear the whispers in the background, but that's because everybody was just as much on edge as I was. "Damn, Remy, where the hell are you?!"

"Oh, they should be pulling up shortly. He called me not a minute ago and said they were close." Wesley said.

"Well, they need to hurry up," I expressed, just as Ralph returned with my jacket.

"Here, put this on," he told me. I put my jacket on but was still hot on the inside. I really felt some kind of way.

"Remy dem pulling up." Wesley pointed.

I took in a deep breath and then slowly let it out. My heart pounded at just the thought of saying what I'd just heard. It couldn't be true but, then again, I kind of got it from the horse's mouth. I was just in total disbelief.

"Yooo!" Remy loudly said, as he jumped out the passenger side of Joe's jeep. "What the hell is going on? Sweets, why you acting so crazy over the phone?"

"Yeah, talk to us," Nana said.

"I mean, this wait is driving me crazy," Natacha added.

"Well," I started with a shake of the head. "I got a collect call from the county jail." I looked over at Remy, as his eyes widened.

"From who?" he pondered.

"Fran."

Everybody looked at me like I was crazy. "I don't understand. Why is Fran calling from the county jail?" Nana asked.

"She's being arrested for murder. Well— conspiracy and murder for hire."

"What?!" Auntie Maddy let out. "Murder for hire?"

"What the fuck?!" Ralph exclaimed. "That can't be right."

"So, she was the woman behind the hit?" Natacha asked but not in an upset tone, just in a *I'm not surprised* kind of tone.

"What hit?" Nana asked, still confused by it all.

"Y'all just chill out for a second. Let me get my thoughts together and I'll explain what she told me when she called."

"Well, you better hurry the hell up because if this got anything to do with my babies, I'm going down to that fuckin' jail and break her lil' ass in two. Do you hear me?!" Nana angrily fussed. "I just know better."

"Well—Nana—" I said, almost feeling sick to my stomach as I leaned over and threw up some of what I'd eaten.

"Sweets!" Remy rushed over. "Just let it out. Just let it out," he said, lightly patting me on the back. Once I gathered my composure, I looked at everyone that was standing there. I knew this was without a doubt going to break their hearts.

"Well—um—from what Fran told me, she's being arrested for the murder of James and Lovely."

"Nooo!" Nana cried out. "She—"

"Nana, please, let me finish," I softly said with tears in my eyes. I just needed to finish. "She told me that it was a lot I didn't know about her life. One being that she had fallen in love with Rod Cannon and that Lil' D is his son."

"What the fuck?!" Ralph let out. "Wow, is this what she was trying to tell me yesterday before she got that text and dipped out in a hurry?"

"Probably," I shrugged, just as Remy's cell phone began to ring. He looked down at the display screen but didn't answer.

"I'm so confused," Aunt Maddy disappointedly said. "So, Fran was dating Rod and had a baby by him. Lil' D is his?" She frowned.

"Yeah, according to Fran."

"Wow, that baby do look like a Cannon. Why didn't we see that before?"

"Because we didn't know before," Wesley cut in. "Man, this some bullshit. I really wish I could choke the life outta Fran right now. She put all this in motion over a nigga that don't want her. That's fucked up!" he yelled. "I wonder if Lovely had found out because of something she'd mentioned to me."

I fell to my knees and cried out like a baby, as everybody gathered around me. Fran was the closest person to me other than my family. We worked together, we hung together, I was her son's God Mama, we were thick as thieves and loved each other wholeheartedly, at least I thought we—she did. She was very cool with Lovely; they would talk about shit that Fran didn't want to tell me. I thought she loved my sister too. She fed my family often, she visited us often— how could she do this us?

"Sweets, come on. Get up," Remy said as his phone rang again. He quickly sent the caller to voicemail. "Get up," he told me. As I stood to my feet, wiping my tears, Natacha reached out and hugged me so tight.

"It's gon' be okay baby. Just trust that it'll be okay."

"Is there anything else she said?" Aunt Maddy asked.

"She said she was sorry and to take care of Lil' D. Wow, his real name is Darius and Rod's name is Rodarius. I never put the two together. I can't believe it. I was the one that told her about Rod and Lovely fuckin' around on the low. I was the one that told her Lovely was pregnant. It's my fault. I caused this."

"No, you didn't," Josette intervened. "You thought she was a friend, not a lowlife bitch that would have our siblings killed. They better keep her in there because if they don't, I'm gon' take her ass out myself."

"This is too much," Nana cried out. "She was like a daughter to me. How could she do this to us?!"

"Mama, please. Just calm down." Auntie said.

Remy's phone kept going off. Finally, it rang again as he looked at us. "This is Nessa. She text and said for me to answer. She got something to tell me involving the Fran."

"Well, answer it," Auntie said.

"Yeah," he answered with the phone on speaker.

"Islande, this is not about Amir being your son—"

"What the fuck?!" Auntie let out. "Did she just say her son is yo' son?"

"I fuckin' knew it," Nana said with a shake of the head. "It's too many secrets around this bitch."

"Y'all hush, damn. Let the woman talk," Remy spat.

"Oh shit, you got me on speaker huh?"

"Yeah, and they heard you."

"Damn," she softly whispered.

"They know now, so ain't no need to hide it no more. Anyway, what you called for?"

"Well, anyway—" she sighed. "Darnell called to tell me that they arrested Fran late last night. Supposedly, she's being charged for murder, really murder to hire or something like that. He said that she hired two boys from Columbine to kill Lovely. Just so happen, Wesley and James was in the car when it happened. However, when she was questioned, she told them that Tony Cannon wanted in and he basically was the one that killed James."

"So, Fran did hire them boys and Tony?"

"Um—he said that she told them that her and Tony had always been cool, and so she ran the plot by him to see what he thought about it. I guess already knowing it was apparent beef between him and James. Well, he wanted it to happen worse than her, so he decided to join the hit."

"Un-fuckin'-believable—" Nana exclaimed. "I don't wanna hear no more. I'm going inside."

"Yeah, you need to relax and take your meds," Auntie said, as she grabbed Nana by the arm and walked her in the house.

"I'm going inside too. This is a lot to take in," Josette angrily expressed.

I just stood up, looking at Remy's phone like I could see Nessa on the other end.

"So, Nessa, are they picking up Tony?" Joe asked. He hadn't said nothing since they pulled up and spoke to everybody. I just felt like he was processing everything that was being said.

"They got him a couple of hours ago. He's in the interrogation room. But Darnell said that he's denying having anything to do with it and is putting everything on the guys from Columbine and Fran."

"Dirty bitch," I let out. "His lyin' muthafuckin' ass. I know he was in on it."

"We all do," Remy said.

"That nigga been hatin' my brother for a long ass time," Joe said. "But I got something for him."

"Oh, um— Islande— Fran told them that she tried to call off the hit the day of, but that Tony took over and decided that they were still going to do it. She said at that point, it was out of her hands," Nessa revealed.

"No, the fuck it wasn't! She could've said something to somebody!" I spat.

"Damn right! I almost got killed too in that bullshit! Fran gon' get hers! Just wait. She gon' get what's coming to her!" Wesley growled.

I glanced over at Natacha. As always, she was quiet as a mouse, but her body language was loud and clear. She wanted some get back. I could see it in her eyes.

"I'm getting cold babe. Can we go in?"

"You can go in, I'm coming," Wesley responded.

As Gaelle walked off, I looked at Remy and just shook my head. I didn't even know what else to say, as Ralph wrapped his arms around me.

"Don't worry love. We'll get through this."

"Nessa, was anything else said that we may need to know about?" I asked.

"Um— oh, she also said that Rod knew nothing about it. He wasn't in on it either."

"That makes me feel a lil' better," Ralph said. "But, technically, he was cheating on Lovely with Fran."

"They were having problems. I knew that. Lovely didn't want to out their relationship but Rod did. He wanted people to know that they were in love. She wanted to hold off," I explained. "Maybe that had something to do with it."

"But it also could've led to him to messing around on her with Fran," Remy concluded with a shrug. "Anything else babe?"

"No but, if I hear something else, I will be sure to call and let you know. Oh, but before you hang up. We still got things to discuss."

"I know. We will," Remy said and ended the call.

"Damn, man, did she say that her son was yours?" Santana asked with a frown. "How the hell? You never told me you made a trip back here."

"That's because I didn't." Everybody looked puzzled. "It's a long story, one that I still ain't fully grasped yet. But we'll talk about that later. How you feeling Sweets?"

"I don't know. I just need to lay down. I have a headache"

"Where's the baby?" Wesley asked.

"He's in the house sleeping," Ralph answered. "Come on love. Let's go in. You need to calm down."

"And you need to call yo' mama and tell her about her bald-headed, grimy ass niece!" I yelled out of nowhere. "Fuckin' bitch! Yo' whole family need to know about that slut bucket bitch! She's lucky I love that baby—"

"Lil' D don't have nothing to do with her behavior," Ralph said.

"I know he don't, and I'll never take nothing out on him, but Francine— that bitch gon' get hers."

"And I can't tell you how to feel about that situation or her. Let's just go inside. It's getting cold out here."

I looked back at everybody that was still standing there and walked off. I had to go inside and clear my thoughts. I was still blown by what I'd found out. I wanted and prayed for answers. I just didn't know it'd hit so close to home. This was something that I probably would never be able to come to terms with, but I knew I had to figure this shit out or it would eat me alive. Plus, Ralph and I had a baby that we'd have to fully take care of now. I also had a restaurant that still needed to stand strong regardless of the circumstances surrounding it.

"Wow, this is some unbelievable shit."

ISLANDE "REMY" PIERRE

7 Months Later...

I fixed me a drink while thinking about the events that had happened over the course of 7 months. Never did I think we would've had to bury my sister and my cousin at the same time. What made that worse was knowing who was behind them getting killed. Francine's thoughts and feelings triggered a whirlwind of reckless actions that could never be taken back. Unfortunately, she got what was coming to her.

As I sat down to sip on a glass of Merlot and watch the season finale of Snowfall, my cell phone rang.

"Sweets, what's happening? How you feeling?"

"I'm good, can't complain," she answered. "I miss you being here."

"I know and I'll be coming back next month."

"Are you planning on moving back since you and Nessa have been rekindling y'all's romantic relationship?"

"Well, we gotta do something being that Mir is now in my life."

"He has stolen my heart. It's days when I still can't believe she kept him from us like that."

"She had her reasons and I've come to understand 'em."

"I feel you," Royal said. "It's good seeing y'all back together. I mean, Amir looks just like you. No wonder she kept him from around us. We would've known the minute we saw him."

"I know, right. That's the same thing I said. I love her and I definitely love him. He loves his daddy too. I mean, it's like from the second she introduced us, he's treated me as if I've always been around."

"Y'all are so adorable around each other. Who would've known that after all these years, Nessa still wanted to have a baby by you? I mean, damn, after all that time that you were gone, she was able to use your sperm and get pregnant without yo' ass. She must really love you."

"That or she just knew no other nigga was gon' create such an amazing lil' boy as Mir."

Royal laughed. "You're so fuckin' arrogant."

"It's the truth." I grinned. "So, what's going on there? How's Nana?"

"Nana is doing well. She's just happy that you're coming home more and that Nessa accepted yo' proposal. For a minute, we didn't think she was going to say yes." She laughed. "But she did and I'm so happy to know that true love does exist, no matter how far the distance or the time a part."

"I'm happy too. She really makes me happy. It's just on such a different level now, which makes it even truer."

"I can see that. I'm happy for y'all."

"Thanks sis."

"Listen, Joe definitely got Nana smiling from ear to ear. I still can't believe he moved back home."

"I know, right. I miss his ass up here. That might be why I visit so much," I teased. "I can't blame him though. I just didn't think he'd move in with Nana."

"Why you think she got this big ass house? Each room has its own private section of square footage. If she could have it her way, we'd all be in this house with her."

"Well, she definitely got enough room, that's for sure."

"Not to mention, the big ass guest house she's building out back. I mean, the damn house gon' have four bedrooms. What kind of guest house is that?"

"I don't know." I laughed. "Nana thinks she's slick. I believe that house is for us."

Royal laughed. "I told her that too."

"What she said?"

"It is if y'all wanna move in it."

I grinned. "I knew it."

"She ain't slick."

"But she thinks she is. So, how are you coping being a full-time mom and holding down the restaurant?"

"Well, Ralph helps me with the baby for the most part. His family is also great with helping us out. Natacha babysits a lot for me when I'm working. You know everybody in this house gon' help out, regardless. That's what our village do for each other anyway."

"Right."

"Fran hasn't been missed much because Greta and Lulu hold down that damn kitchen and they've been training new hires, as well. We have all the recipes that Fran left behind. Plus, before she hung herself in that cell, she had written me a letter on where to go and get that recipe book she had put up. It was a lot of things that she had planned and that she wanted to add to the menu over time. So, that gave us a leg up that we need now and in the future. I guess in a way that was her trying to make sure that the restaurant stayed on top."

"Damn, not to cut you off, but that's crazy how she ended up hanging herself."

"I know, right. I still think about it a lot. I know it's been three months now, but it seems like yesterday when I got the phone call. I guess she couldn't handle serving life in prison. Plus, she had already gotten shanked right before she took her own life. People 'round here was angry with her about that shit. I figured somebody was going to take her out eventually anyway, but I guess she beat 'em to it."

"That's wild."

"Yeah, but she asked for that. I can't even feel sorry for her. I only feel bad that Lil' D won't get the chance to know who his real mama is and, when the day comes for me to talk about her, I won't even know what I'll say."

"I know but, when that day comes, you'll have it figured out."

"Yeah, I hope so," he said, just as I heard Nessa and my lil' man coming in.

"Well, Nessa just got here."

"You didn't tell me she was flying out that way."

"She decided she'd come last minute."

"That's what folks do when they got a billion dollars laying around," Royal teased.

"Stop it. You know I have assets and investments. I don't just have a billion dollars laying around, but I am worth a billion, that's for sure."

"Yeah, and y'all live like it. Taking trips to Dubai for three weeks then returning to go to Sea World and Disney for two weeks. Hell, aren't you taking her to Africa and Greece next month for y'all's honeymoon? I can't wait to babysit Mir while y'all are gone."

"Hell yeah, and I can't wait, either. I've even thought about just waking up and flying out to Vegas and getting the shit over with. I want— Need her in my life like the air I breathe."

"Oh, hell nawl. You owe her this big lavish ass wedding— Shit, you owe us too."

I laughed. "You're right and she's going to get all of that. This is just the beginning."

"Awww, never thought I'd hear you talking like this."

"I know, right."

"Daddy!" Amir shrieked the minute he entered the family room. He was always so chipper when he saw me.

"Hey, my handsome boy," I cheesed as Mir jumped in my arms. "A'ight sis. We'll catch up later."

"Okay, tell Nessa I said hey and kiss Mir for me."

"I gotcha." I smiled, as she ended the call.

"Hey, my soon to be hubby." Nessa smiled as she joined us, kissing me softly on the lips.

"Hey, my love. You look good with yo' sexy, pretty tail self."

"Thank you." She blushed while giggling.

"I'm glad you flew out here. I missed y'all."

"You know we can't stay away from each other too long. We gotta do something about this living situation. We're always back and forth, but I wanna get stable in one spot and just travel when necessary or wanted."

"I agree." I nodded. "So, check this out. Santana called to gush over his relationship. I think he's found the one. Him and Shakita been getting real close lately."

"Well—if you must know. She just told me that she's six weeks pregnant."

My eyes stretched wide open. "What the hell?"

"Yeah, that's the same thing I said."

"It must be baby making season because Wes and Gaelle are expecting too."

"I know, right. I thought about them when Kita told me the news."

"My boy must don't know because he would've told me that. I just talked to him about an hour ago."

"Nawl, she wanna surprise him, so don't say nothing."

"I'm not. He's definitely gonna be surprised, though. Damn, I'm happy for them. I'm gon' be another uncle." I grinned.

"That you are." She smiled. "And I'm gon' be an auntie."

"Oh, yeah, Sweets told me to tell you hey."

"Every time I think about her, I think about Fran. It's a shame how she ended up going out."

"I know, right. But my sister has picked up those pieces and doing well for herself."

"As she should, and I'm proud of her for that."

"Me too. I just still can't believe that muthafucka Tony got off with just a slap on the wrist. But he'll get his in due time too. Revenge is a dish best served cold."

"As long as you don't have nothing to do with it, I'm good. We got a lot to lose. You can't be getting yo' ass in no trouble."

"I know that babe. I won't," I said as she shot me the side-eye. "I promise."

"Okaaay," she sang with a playful roll of the eyes. "Well, it's getting late. Mir, you ready to take a bath and get ready for bed?"

"Yes ma'am," he responded.

"Give me kiss," I told him. He did just that, as I tickled him a bit before putting him down. I just loved to hear his laughter.

"Come on baby." Nessa smiled, then directed her attention at me. "Be ready for some snuggle time by the time I'm done. It's pouring cats and dogs out there. All I wanna do is lay in your arms."

"And that's all I want you to do." I winked.

As they headed upstairs, my cell phone rang. I glanced at the caller ID to see that it was Joe. Quickly, I answered. "Yooo, wassup my nigga?"

"Aye, you busy?"

"Nawl, wassup?"

"You won't believe what happened not too long ago."

"What?" I nosily pondered.

"Tony Cannon's house just burned down. A bitch went live as they stood around recording the shit."

"Who was recording it?"

"Some lil' young jits in the neighborhood."

"Damn," I uttered.

"Word is he was in that bitch when it happened."

"Nooooo, you gotta be kidding me." A part of me felt disappointed that I didn't get to be the one to wipe that smirk off his face.

"Nawl, I believe it's true because I hear Royal on her phone now. I think she's talking to Rod."

"Find out."

"Hold on," Joe said.

I sipped from my drink, impatiently waiting. I knew damn well that nigga ain't go out like that. He was supposed to have a different fate.

"Cuz."

"Wassup Joseph."

"It's true. Rod just told Royal that he was home when it happened."

"Damn, that's wild yo."

"I know right but, hey, looks like him and Fran got what was coming to them. Can't fuck people over and think you're going to get away with it."

"Like cuz used to say, don't fuck with the Pierres or the Baptistes."

Joe grinned. "Damn, I miss my brother."

"I know. We all do. Lovely would be so happy to know I have a son. I missed out being the uncle that spoiled her little one. I miss them both so much."

"I know, but they're smiling down on us now. They're guiding us. They're with us every day."

"That's the only thing that keeps me sane."

"Well, I ain't gon' hold ya cuz. I just had to call and tell you that. I'm bout to call and tell Wes now. He gon' be happy as hell to hear this shit."

I grinned. "That's because he's been wanting his get back for months. We just made him realize otherwise," I said, not wanting to say too much. But we knew that time was of essence. We couldn't retaliate right away.

"You're right."

"But we'll talk later," I said. "Oh, but how is Iesha and the girls since moving there?"

"They love it. All this shit we putting out here on this land got they asses not wanting leave, not even to go shopping."

I grinned. "I figured as much. Give 'em all my love till I return. "Kiss Nana for me. Tell her I'll call her in the morning."

"Will do bro."

"A'ight, love you Joe." I could tell he was smiling through the phone, as we ended the call.

After hanging up, I sat puzzled like a muthafucka. How the hell did this nigga's house just suddenly catch on fire with him in it? That was strange as hell to me. It really sounded like a job that needed to be handled and it was, but by who? There was only one person in mind that I could point the finger at. Quickly, I called her phone. She answered on the first ring and what she said told me everything I needed to know.

"My babies can rest in peace now. I Love you son." After saying that, she hung up.

"Wow," I mumbled. Not only was Natacha responsible for Tony's death but, without a doubt, I felt that she also had something to do with Fran's. Ain't no way that woman just hung herself. Ain't no way. For some reason, I smiled. She'd more than proven her love, and that was all I ever needed and wanted from her. I hated it had to be shown in that manner but, at this point, I'd take it however it came about. She was the real gangster here and, because of that, I'd always respect her to the fullest.

I flipped off the tv and grabbed the bottle of Merlot. All I wanted to do was lie next to my fiancée and enjoy the night. In due time, she was going to be my wife and I couldn't wait. She was indeed my forever and always, and I was going to make sure that she and Mir never wanted for nothing in this lifetime and beyond.

The End...

Up Next...

FROM THE TRAP HOUSE TO THE PENTHOUSE part 2... catch up with part 1 if you haven't already. Be on the lookout. Thanks for reading. I hope you enjoyed it.

If you're in need of a total relaxation while preparing to read and reset mentally, head on over to The Spiritual Tea Company to get your fix of body butters, spiritual bath soaks, meditation baths, body teas, bath bombs, sugar scrubs, sage, manifestation candles, spiritually lit candles & more. You won't be disappointed. Surround yourself with positive energy and good vibes. You got this! (www.thespiritualteacompany.com)

Asè

Other Books Written by Tiece...

*Property Of A Hood Millionaire 1-4 Complete Series

*Just Can't Leave Him Alone 1-5, Originally Titled, CheckMate (Complete Series)

*I Need Love 1-4, Originally Titled, SCARLETT (Complete Series) also, Available in a 4-book boxset

*Falling In Love with The Goat 1-3 (Complete Series) also, Available in a 3-book Box Set

*Ms. Thang and The Connect 1-2 (Compléte Series) also, Available in a 2-book Box Set

*Thug Me Good & Lie To Me 1 & 2 (Complete Series)

*Drunk in Love 1-4 (Complete Series) also, Available in a 4-book boxset

*Woman To Woman 1-3 (Complete Series) also, Available in a 3-book Boxset

*Rich Boy Thuggin' Is A Whole Vibe (A Complete Novel)

*My Girl Got a Girlfriend (A Complete Novel)

*Shorty Found Love With a Dope Boy (A Complete Novel)

*The First Wife 1-3 (Part 4 still in the works)

*Shanice Capone's Truth, A Shorty Story (Located at the end of The First Wife part 3)

*Southern Gossip 1-2

*It's Either Me Or Her 1-2

*Crushin' On A Down South Boss; 1- & 2 Coming Soon.

*Classy & Ratchet, Originally Titled, Ratchet Bitches 1-2

*Dopeboyz & the Women That Love 'em

*A Boss Valentine In Atlanta (A Short Story)

*These Games We Play

*He Needed Her Savage Love

*For The Love Of My Trap King 1-2 Originally Titled, Shawty Is My Rock (A completed Series, Will be turned into a Standalone Novel)

My Catalog is continually being updated with each New Release, Title Change, or Boxset Release... Stay Woke...

Made in the USA
Monee, IL
20 May 2022